HAPPY BABY

HAPPY BABY

BY

STEPHEN ELLIOTT

MacAdam/Cage

McSWEENEY'S BOOKS
826 Valencia Street
San Francisco, CA 94110

www.mcsweeneys.net

MACADAM/CAGE PUBLISHING
155 Sansome Street, Suite 550
San Francisco, CA 94104

www.macadamcage.com

"My Wife" was originally published as "Did Something Happen" in the
Alaska Quarterly. "Stalking Gracie" and "Where You Could End" were
originally published in the *Sun*. "The Yard," "Getting In Getting Out," and
"Listen" were originally published as "I'll Change Completely" in *McSweeney's*.
"Stop First" was originally published in *Fourteen Hills*.
"Stevenson House" was originally published in *Center*.

Cover art by Amelia Bauer.

This book is a work of fiction.

ISBN: 1-93-156162-1

Also by the author

NOVELS

What It Means to Love You
A Life Without Consequences
Jones Inn

AS EDITOR

Politically Inspired

Dedicated to the state of Illinois

I don't know why somebody becomes one way and someone else becomes another way. Say you have ten dogs, or five dogs, and you beat the dogs and you kick them. A couple of dogs are gonna get really vicious and they're gonna be like, vicious killer dogs, and then maybe one or two are going to be crazy. And one of them will be a little crazy but also kind of always looking for affection, and really loyal to the person that beats them.

JT LEROY, FROM AN INTERVIEW

MARIA HAS A CHILD

IT'S A HALF-EMPTY early morning flight from Oakland into Midway and the sun is coming up, lighting the plane like the inside of an eyelid. The stewardess asks in a whisper if I would like another coffee and I say OK and she sets it on the tray with a white napkin and a small bag of cheese- flavored pretzels, which I stuff in the pouch with the others. I reach over my head and turn the light off. The plane is glowing, there's so much sun outside. I'm in the back and I have all three seats. I haven't been in Chicago in six years and I've only been on a plane three times in my life. I don't like to fly.

There's a giant sound like a bird has been sucked into one of the jets and the seatbelt light flashes on. I grip the armrests as the plane shakes violently twice then continues its course. The pilot doesn't say anything over the speakers and most of the passengers stay asleep. I turn and see the stewardess in the dark back cabin, sitting in a triangle of light, on a platform against a series of metal cases, reading a magazine, the belt across her lap unfastened. I have blisters on both hands where my girlfriend,

1

Ambellina, burned me with a cigarette when I told her I was going to Chicago for the weekend. I brought just a small bag with me, a change of clothes, a notebook, and an alarm clock. I'm traveling light.

Chicago has changed. Midway is a big airport now and there's a train that rides all the way to downtown. Hallways as long as boulevards lead to a food court offering soaked beef sandwiches and Vienna hot dogs. The new Mayor Daley welcomes me home, his face plastered across a billboard in front of the train station. I want to climb the scaffolding and kiss him and tell him I'm glad to be back here, even for just a little while. There's a look in the mayor's eyes, both knowing and sinister. Chicagoans prefer their politicians crooked and I can understand why. Whatever he has to do, he looks like the guy for the job.

At the Loyola train stop I board the Devon bus and pass Clark Street, where the diners are still painted like Indian casinos, tomahawks and dollar signs over plates full of fried eggs and chili fries. The bus passes Carrie's, which I didn't expect to still be there, but it is, an Irish bar in the middle of a Muslim neighborhood. Then Western Avenue, Hobby Models now a luggage store, the Nortown theater replaced with a Pakistani assembly hall. Little India, traffic pauses. I lay my head against the glass, and the slow rocking of the bus nearly puts me to sleep. Shirnee bob in pans full of syrup in the windows. I get off the bus to walk.

Almost immediately the strap of my bag whips tight against my neck. "Don't I know you, motherfucker?" I turn to face a man six-and-a-half feet tall with enormous sloping shoulders, his head like an anvil with a bald stripe running down the center of it, a necklace of tattoos partially obscured by the collar of his denim jacket. His clothes are torn and his face smeared in acne and weeping sores.

"I don't think so."

"Give me a dollar."

We stand for a second. His nose is like a bull's and pulses while he breathes. His lips peel back to reveal cracked brown teeth and spangled gums. He balls his fists and releases a low growl. The foot traffic continues around us as if nothing is happening. This is where I grew up.

"I'm just kidding," he says, his cracked lips retreating into a smile. "You don't know me, man. Don't look so scared."

And he turns and walks away, the dirty frays on the bottom of his jeans brushing the sidewalk.

After California Avenue the bright colors are gone and things get quieter. Three Orthodox Jews stand in the rubble parking lot of a synagogue reading to each other and swaying beneath the chipped wooden sign of a star and sickle.

Thillen's Stadium is still there, where the Little Leaguers play next to the canal. Brown's Chicken has been replaced by Fried USA. There's the Lincoln Bridge, which I won't cross, but on the other side of the bridge is Lincoln Village and Shadows Nightclub, its sign divided into great black wings spread against the facade. I won't go over there. I can see from where I'm standing that they've built new movie theaters and a car wash. The old mall has been scrubbed and painted into a shiny metropolis and it hides the cheap motels on the other side of it. The bridge is city limits. After the bridge you're not in Chicago anymore.

I knock on apartment No. 10 on the third floor of a three-story rail flat. All of the apartments share a long cement porch and the view is of a closed-down gas station and a deli. One of the apartments has half a dozen pots full of dead plants outside of its door, another a bicycle frame with no wheels. At the end of the porch a man is having a cigarette; he doesn't look at me when I knock. A woman comes outside, her head wrapped in a scarf and says something to the man but he keeps his back to her and she goes back inside. He pitches his cigarette out to the gutter and takes a pouch of tobacco from his pocket and slowly rolls another one.

"Well," Maria says when she answers the door, a little at first and then all the way, a baby cradled in her arm. She laughs, then I laugh. God she's beautiful. She steps out to the porch and the man on the end turns to regard her. The child stretches its arms and squeezes its tiny fists as if waking from a nap. I look past her to see if the apartment is empty. Then her face, which hasn't changed much, long and oval like an egg. A little older and fatter. Her breasts are larger and she has curves I can make out even beneath her baggy clothes. She's wearing a striped shirt, two buttons open, and blue jeans. She's wearing them in a comfortable way, bunched all the way to her ankles and low on her hips, like she doesn't care how they look. Her dark cheeks are almost pink but she isn't wearing any makeup. I wasn't expecting her to have a baby. The baby changes everything.

"You show up at the oddest times," she says, which makes me smile even more, thinking about the last time, ten years ago, when her boyfriend threw me out of a bar.

"It's only three o'clock," I say, wondering how it took so long to get here.

"Very funny, Dumbo. You know what I mean."

We're seated at her kitchen table drinking tea. The baby's name is Kyle. It's a small one- bedroom apartment, like a studio with doors, but a lot larger than the place she and I used to live in. There's an enormous box of corn flakes above the fridge, three pans of different sizes dangling over the stove. She has a couch, a small stereo shaped like a jukebox, some toys on the floor, and one entire wall filled with paperback books.

"What happened to your hands?" Maria asks. The blisters are the size of pencil erasers. I had forgotten my burns. I think she would understand if I told her. Ambellina was jealous; she gets that way. I look down at the muscles between my thumbs and index fingers, push my thumbs against my fingers. Ambellina didn't want me to go but I told her I had to so she pulled my hand toward her, locking my elbow between her knees, pushing my palm into her leg. I said no and she said yes, pressing the cigarette into the back of my wrist, making a sound like the sizzle of an opium pipe. I screamed. "Now the other one," she said.

"Bacon grease," I tell Maria. "It's nothing."

"Both hands?"

"I know."

"I don't know," she says, patting her child. She lives here alone. There's no evidence of anyone else in this apartment, a small dish of baby food perched on the edge of the sink. The runners are tan and the paint is chipped, revealing an older layer of blue paint beneath it.

When I first met Maria we were fifteen and both living in state homes for wards of the court. All the boys were playing basketball when the van from the girls' home arrived. She was just admitted, wearing all pink: pink shoes, pink earrings, pink shorts and shirt. She looked like an unopened piece of candy. She was shy and scared but I knew something horrible had happened to her because girls don't often end up in group homes. We made a lot of promises then, about staying together and looking out for each other. Or maybe I made all the promises, about protecting her and keeping her safe.

"Don't look at me like that," she says, reaching to the counter for the bottle.

"Sorry."

She has an arm around Kyle's waist, her head tilted toward the baby's crown. Kyle has his little hands on the bottle.

"He's like a little person," I say.

"Except he knows what he wants." I stare at the baby, a pile of creases between rings of fat. His skin is the color of eggnog; he has enormous ears.

I notice Maria isn't wearing any rings but that doesn't mean anything. I can see the top of her bra where her shirt is unbuttoned. I was married once, before Ambellina. Ambellina has children I've never met. A girl and a boy. But sometimes just a girl. Ambellina's story changes from time to time. I'm sure she has a daughter, because the girl comes up again and again. I've heard the stories change from grammar school to high school in the time I've been with her.

Kyle has little brown hairs, curly and soft, different from Maria's black hair, which has always been straight and dry. The two of them are smiling. I wonder how much time she spends here, speaking with her baby, and if she talks to anyone else. She turns the child around so he faces me, his fat little belly hanging over his diapers, his mouth open, waiting for some more good news, the bridge of her hands under his arms. The baby is directly between us. I lean back in my chair, fingers on the cup handle. I thought Maria would be alone or she would be married but I didn't expect this. Two smiling faces. The pale baby, his mouth the shape of a firecracker with a wick on both ends. Maria, her dark cheeks flushed. That could have been our child. He's not even a year old. I would have named him Kyle too, if that's what she wanted.

"Tell me something," Maria says.

"I live in San Francisco now. Every day it's the same temperature. My girlfriend didn't want me to come here."

"Maybe you should have listened to her," Maria says. "I'm just teasing. You want some more tea?"

"Sure. It's good tea."

"Hold on a second. Let me get this pot going again. And let me change this little guy." Maria keeps Kyle against her as she reaches over the stove light. Maria used to be skinny. She used to starve herself.

There's a couple of clicks as the flame pops beneath the kettle. She leans her hip into the cabinet and lays Kyle on top of a towel on the counter, pulls the pin out of his diaper. Kyle kicks his legs like he's riding a bicycle.

"This isn't a bad place," I say. "Bigger than my place. I live on a busy street and dirt comes through the window from the exhaust. There's a factory across the street where they make fancy chocolates but you wouldn't know it looking at the sidewalks at night. I'm thinking about moving somewhere nicer." I scratch my head.

"Hand me one," she says, lifting Kyle, pointing to a box. I get up and grab her a diaper then sit back down. The old diaper goes in a sack held with two rods. She wipes Kyle and fastens the new diaper around his legs.

"How about you?"

"About me?" Maria begins. "I still live in Chicago."

"Ha ha."

"Well, there was Joe. That's most of it. You met him."

"I did. I met him the hard way."

"Everybody met Joe the hard way." I bring the cup back to my lips before realizing it's empty. "Hey, I'm sorry. I shouldn't have let him do that."

"It was out of your hands."

"I can't even tell you. I loved him the most."

I feel something drop and put the cup down harder than I mean to. I don't think I ever doubted for a day that I loved Maria the most. My wife knew that. She could sense it. I love Ambellina too, but it's different. On my last day in the group home, Maria and I were in the smoking room waiting for the car that was going to take me to a place called Prairie View. I was almost seventeen and I would have done anything for Maria. My hand was inside her shirt, fiddling with the bottom of her bra, feeling the weight of her breasts. She slid her leg over my legs and then to the other side of me and I was on top of her on the couch. We were waiting for that car and it felt like we had all the time in the world but we used it as best we could. I don't know if staff heard us or not. But no one came to the door.

"Don't look at me that way either," she says. "You look like a wolf."

Kyle starts to cry. I turn away for a second. It's an awful sound. The kettle is ringing and the room is filling with steam. Maria reaches over and shuts the stove off, the pot rattling across the burner.

"Let's give the baby some attention," she says. "Let's all look at the baby. Who's the baby? Are you the baby? Everybody loves the baby. Everybody listens to the baby when the baby cries." She's bouncing Kyle and soon Kyle is happy again. It seems so easy.

Maria pours tea into my cup. She's still holding Kyle with one arm. The cup full, she keeps the pot near to my hand. "I've had burns like those," she says. "They're going to scar. First they'll become like little craters on your wrist. Then, as they heal, they'll leave pale round marks. I have eight of them on my right thigh. Starting on my knee and finishing at my waist.

They're like buttons."

I stare at her middle, try to imagine her new scars beneath her clothes. "What are we talking about?"

"I was telling you my story."

I hide my hands in my lap for a moment until she looks away.

"How did you find me, by the way?" she asks, placing the kettle back on the stove and taking her seat across from me but holding Kyle so his face is just above the table, his tiny hands gripping the edge.

"I see you," I say to Kyle. He grins at me. "People aren't that hard to find. You can find anybody now for fifty dollars. You were telling me about Joe."

"Yes, Joe. I lived with Joe for years. He always took care of me. This is what I think. That some people, they get what they want, it just makes them want more. He was a violent person."

"That's one way of putting it."

"He never hurt me too much."

"How would you know?"

"Don't joke. They gave him fifty years." She's quiet for a second and the baby is still. In the silence I hear voices coming from the wall. It's her neighbors having a conversation about soup. She smiles awkwardly when she realizes what I'm listening to. "He had two strikes already for some other things. He strangled a man outside of the Oak Club. I saw him do it. They had said something to each other. Joe was the bouncer. I never got the full story. Everybody has a different view of the situation. Sometimes Joe would kick somebody out just to have a fight."

She takes Kyle in both hands again and bounces him up and down. I wish she would stop playing with the baby. He yells and claps. I wait for her to continue while she pulls Kyle toward her and he stretches his arm out and she takes his fist in her mouth

Then she opens her mouth and he takes his arm back. She turns in her chair and crosses her legs.

"You're spoiling him," I say.

"That's OK. One of us needs to be spoiled. Makes up for the cheap diapers. Anyway, this guy. You know I would let Joe do anything he wanted. I wanted him to do whatever he wanted to me. I tried to cover the bruises with makeup. My caseworker wanted to put me in a woman's shelter to get me away from him, so I stopped meeting with her and lost my SSI. I didn't care what she thought. But he needed more. Hence the bacon grease."

Maria reaches across the table to touch the blisters near my fingers. They're raised and yellow with pink halos around them.

"Wait. Don't do anything." She touches the blister carefully. "Joe wanted to hurt people; he couldn't help it." I can feel the bubble of liquid move just a little bit under her pressure. Her finger glides along the top of the blister. "He would pierce me with things. He carved his name into my back with a scalpel and covered it with baking soda so it wouldn't heal. I could show you." She waits for an answer.

"No. I'm not interested."

"Fine. People don't think that's love. But listen, this is important. If you pop these you have to cover them with Bacitracin and a Band-Aid. You have to watch out for infection. But you shouldn't pop them. They'll heal better if you don't." I nod my head. "Promise me."

"Sure."

"Liar." Maria continues to look at the blisters. "OK. Joe is standing up and he has his hands around this guy's throat. And the guy is turning blue. And people are pulling on Joe's arms, trying to get him to let go. But Joe worked out six days a week;. He only ate red meat. One guy was literally hanging from Joe's arm with his full weight. But nobody could get him to let go.

He still had the guy's neck when the police came. There were three cars surrounding Joe. I thought they were going to bull-doze him into the bar. Those police, with their guns, you could tell they were scared."

"A badge doesn't change that."

"I wouldn't testify and they threatened to lock me up for contempt of court. They came around here. They said they had a warrant but I didn't ask to see it and the only place they searched was the refrigerator. They didn't need me—there were dozens of witnesses. Finally they left me alone."

I wonder how she pays the rent here. Maria took our savings with her when she left me, a couple of hundred dollars, but she left her clothes, and the apartment continued to smell like her for a long time. This is a small apartment to have a child in—a little front room, the kitchen part of the living room, a television set with a towel over the front of it. A cable sticking out of the wall not connected to anything. Hundreds of paperback books, the kind you get in a grocery store. A bedroom I can see from here, just big enough for a pine bed and a dresser. But there's no crib. She must sleep with Kyle, so if he wakes up crying she's there right behind him, her breasts and her stomach. I bet he goes right back to sleep. I bet he has no idea how small the apart-ment is that he's living in because she doesn't let him know.

"He's not Joe's child, is he?"

"No. He's not. He's only my child."

"Can I hold him?"

"In a little while. Not just yet."

I stay for the day with Maria and Kyle. We take a walk down a side street to the park. The weather is perfect for it. The park is empty. There's only one basketball rim there now. There used to be two, and a light. Probably the neighbors complained about the children playing basketball at night. The sun is almost down and we're sitting on a brown bench in front of a sprinkler-fountain when Maria hands me Kyle. He feels like a doll filled with jelly and he weighs more than I thought he would. My wife almost had a baby twice. After that there wasn't any chance of anything working out.

I hold Kyle so he's standing on my leg. I squeeze his belly with my thumbs. He smiles at me, his face cocked to the side. He looks curious. I won't try to spend the night with Maria. I wouldn't want to interrupt the two of them. Two older boys come running past us, one of them boys carrying a crowbar and the other laughing. They're together, running after someone else we can't see.

"You ever go to visit Joe?" I ask.

"He's in Marion," she says and I nod. "But that's not why I don't want to visit him. He wouldn't like Kyle. So maybe I'm wrong to say I love him the most. A mother doesn't love anybody more than her baby."

"A good mother."

"Most mothers."

"Some mothers."

Maria laughs. "God, you can be cynical. I write Joe letters. I edit Kyle out. Actually, I make up the letters. I write him fictional stories where I'm at the gym and I'm working out all the time with his old friends. I tell him he has a fan club back here and everybody misses him. I tell him about a friend I made up. Joannie. I say Joannie and I went to the movies today and a man offered to buy her popcorn. It doesn't matter. There's no chance of parole in this state. It's not like I'm going to see him again."

Across from the park on one side is a row of identical houses. The houses are new. On the other side of the park each house is different and in front of one a woman in a long dress has come outside barefoot to water her lawn. Two doors down from her there is a house that looks abandoned, the slats untreated and rotting, the yard overgrown with weeds. There's trash in the plants, cups sitting on branches. The mailbox hangs upside down, its lid gaping open. In place of a buzzer two wires protrude from a hole next to the door. I look a little harder and see a face behind a curtain. The house isn't abandoned at all.

I hand Kyle back to Maria and she stands him on her leg. "Who's the baby," she says to him again. "You're still the baby aren't you? The baby needs attention."

It's after dark, but the weather hasn't changed. I don't remember the weather being this nice in Chicago when I was here. The weather is so flawless right now you can't even feel it. I remember Chicago as always too hot or too cold.

I leave Kyle and Maria at the door to her apartment. She stands in the doorframe and I stand back at the rail with my bag over my shoulders. I could fly back or I could spend a day visiting my old schools and places. Maybe go to the top of the Sears Tower and look out over Chicago, check out the lake and the condominiums at the end of Lake Shore Drive where my wife's boyfriend lived. But if I get home early maybe I can see Ambellina tomorrow. I think she's actually worried that I won't come back.

"I could put you in a cage," Ambellina said. I was lying with my head in her lap and she was stroking my hair. She had hiked her skirt up and her bare legs were warm. I was naked and wet, fresh from the shower. "I could take you back to my house and lock you in the basement. Then where would you go?" Her finger brushed against my ear and she gently squeezed my nose shut. Then she started crying because she knew. She knew before

I did. I'm not going back.

"It was nice to see you again," Maria says. I almost tell her I have another day, then catch myself. I have as many more days as I want, but that's not the point. Maria's safe, she didn't need me after all. Kyle has his back turned to me, resting, sleeping I think, in Maria's collar. He could be rising from her skin, he blends in so perfectly. I look from his back to her face. The view from that apartment we shared in Jonquil twenty years ago, how different that was, across from a playground where the smaller kids kept watch from monkeybars for the dope dealers waiting between cars. People who came to see you never came inside your building but waited for you down on the street instead. How quiet it is, only three miles away. I can feel the burns below my thumbs when I rub my thumbs and forefingers together. They hurt now but soon they'll start to itch.

"It's not so late," I say. "Maybe we could go to Campbell and have Chinese food or something."

"No. It's getting near this guy's bedtime. Anyway, we have food here."

Maria slides her arm up to Kyle's waist. I take in as deep a breath as I can and reach out to Maria. She inches forward just a small step and I touch her elbow through her shirt. "All right then," I say.

"So you're going back to San Francisco? Is that your home now?"

Maria still wears the same lotion, peach. It's not so different from Ambellina's but Ambellina has a thicker scent. Ambellina's larger than me. When she lies on top of me I disappear.

"No," I say. "I'm going to run away one more time. I've got one left in me."

"You're not actually a runaway. Or you weren't before, anyway," Maria says.

"It's just a word. The only times I ever regretted it was when I went back." I rub my thumb along her forearm. I lift my hand to her chin, my burn touching her face. Kyle doesn't move at all. He'll outgrow this place and then what will they do? In a flash I wish I was violent and capable of the things people are capable of when they don't care whether or not they get caught. There would be blood everywhere. The baby is sound asleep. It's not fair, I think. No, of course it is.

CHAPTER TWO
LISTEN

JUST PROMISE ME your devotion.

Sometimes when my phone rings I try to hide in my own apartment. I close the blinds. The phone rings in the front of the studio near the window and I crawl toward the end of my mattress, where the walls meet. When the phone stops ringing I go to check who it is. It's always her.

Early in the morning before I leave for work, I press the play button on the answering machine. Ambellina's thick, steady voice wakes me.

Understand that this decision was hastened by the feeling I get that you need someone to offer protection, love, and discipline. I know that you're afraid. But I will keep you safe. Honesty is so important in this relationship. I don't do things in halves. You can call me when you feel jealous, uncertain, or insecure. Please arrange to meet me on Saturday. You can lay your head in my lap then.

* * *

"Any letters from your girlfriend?" Valerie asks. It's 6:45 in the morning. I have a headache. I hate myself. We're on the two Internet kiosks in the front of the store. The small round tables have all been wiped down and the blue rags thrown in the sink. The newspapers are stacked beneath the advertisements taped to the wall next to the coffee lids. The bagels are sitting in baskets on three slanted shelves behind the glass.

"Shut up," I say. "Put on the coffee." Valerie has pink hair and she likes to get high. We've worked together in this bagel shop for three years now. This is the question she always asks and this the answer I always give her, to get up, to change the cauldrons, to unbolt the front door and invite in another working day.

Valerie bounces to Sly and the Family Stone as our first customers arrive, spinning around the large square cutting block. "Do you think it's better to play bass or drums?" she asks. "Because if you play bass then you're in front and everybody sees you. But if you play drums you stay in shape and let out all that anger."

"Bass," I tell her.

The first orders are to-go, toasted rolls, egg bagels with dill cream cheese, tall coffees and lattes for people scrambling to trains. Later, people start to sit down. We put the tubs back in the refrigerator. Valerie switches the music to '80s New Wave. "Such a wonderful problem," she sings, raising her fists over her head, swinging them forward from her elbows. "Oh please let me help you."

There are two rooms in the shop and a thin hallway between them. The workers, students, and professionals sit in front near the windows. The junkies and the criminals sit in the back and we let them. They hang out by the fire exit and the restroom with the hookers from Folsom Street who break into the bins in front of the chocolate factory at night. The prison bus stops only two blocks away. The dealers hang out on 16th Street and two doors down in the shooting gallery. I stare at them while pouring the beans into the grinder. The click of the phone. The cauldrons lean forward. The whir of the machine crushing the beans. The tap of the espresso filter. The junkies nod toward the Formica. Valerie's boyfriend, Philc, hangs back there with them, juggling ketchup packets, mini-hypodermics hanging from his ears, wearing a thick spiked collar around his neck. He's always dirty. He likes to brag about his skills with a knife. He says he was a knife thrower with the circus. He sleeps in the shopping cart encampment under the overpass. He steals from the junkies when they sleep.

Ambellina comes to my apartment at 8 p.m. She makes me nervous and shy. I've washed the smell of coffee and lox from my hair, cleaned beneath my nails. I've changed clothes. There's a bowl of caramel popcorn on the table because that's what she likes.

"My husband knows," she says. She walks deliberately, one boot in front of the other. "Yeah, I told him."

She sits on the couch, leans forward first with her fists on her knees and then leans back as I assume my position. She's eating the popcorn. She's drinking white wine from my only glass. Between the small couch and the table I am on the floor on my knees with my head in her lap. "You don't mind, do you? That he knows?"

I shake my head, rub my cheek on the fabric of her skirt, feel her fingers moving on my head. She wants me to be jealous and yanks my head by my hair. I breathe heavily when her grip tightens and she twists her knuckles, sending small pins of pain along my skull. My mouth opens. "What?" she asks. She slaps me. "What do you want to say?" she asks, letting go of my hair and reclining. I stare into her chest, the lines on the country of her body. "My husband doesn't want you to see these." She pushes her breasts together with her forearms. "That's what he asked. These are his favorite." She puckers her lips. She's wearing a thin black negligee. When she's not holding them her breasts slide toward her elbows. They are big, but not firm. More importantly, I don't care about her husband. "Look at me," she says. "Look at me." Ambellina has a broad face and a wide, flat nose, clipped curly hair dyed maroon. "You're pouting." I nod. "Didn't I tell you I would protect you? What are you so worried about?" Her hands are large. Everything about her is large. I close my eyes then the slaps come, back and forth, until I cry, and still more. "Shut up," she hisses. "Shut up. Don't cry. Don't cry. You're mine. Don't cry." And when she stops and her hand slides away from my face I lower my head. I duck carefully toward her. I try to burrow into her, under her skirt, to be inside of her. It's still early. There will be hours more of this. And I will pretend to be jealous of her husband, who may or may not exist. Because it's important to her that I be jealous, so I am, because she likes it.

I met Ambellina two weeks ago on an online personals board for people with Other Desires. A website filled with leather-clad professionals who charge more for an hour than I make in a week, and lonely housewives who say they want to *try something new*. The boards use black backgrounds and are suggestive of something wild. A whip hangs in the left corner of the screen. They give you a form to fill out when you join. They ask you what you're into: eurologia (piss play), collar and lead, smothering, vibrators, pain, asphyxiaphilia (breath play), amputees, electro-torture, fisting, tongues, ears, feet, crossdressing, humiliation, 24/7, cling film, erotic email exchange, cock and ball torture. The list goes on and on. They ask your role: dominant, submissive, switch. They ask how often you think about the lifestyle.

Twice a week they send you Love Dog Reports. It's all angles, women next to punching bags, free pornographic sites that aren't free. Everybody wants to know your real email so they can put you on their list. It's mostly men using the site. There are discussion boards and the men's names are blue and the women's pink and couples are green, but even the women are most likely men. And then Ambellina, who posted no picture and whose ad read *East Bay Woman looking for a toy to abuse. Must be full time. No equivocating.* And I responded by saying I would be her toy, full time. I sent her a picture. I said that she would be my only commitment and I didn't think she would respond but she did.

And the bookstores with all of their trade paperbacks and Eric Stanton artwork saying that it's OK to be weird, to accept who we are. It's fun, they say, to play during sex. To tie each other up and take control. It's just sex. It's just a game. Trade places, let off some steam. I was raped the first time by a middle- aged caseworker in a small green room in the Chicago juvenile detention facility. The windows were closed and the room was dusty and hot and filled with stacks of yellowing, creased paper forced into wide brown envelopes. Mr. Gracie didn't ask me if it was OK and he didn't apologize afterward. When I masturbate at night I think of him and his malty smell. And that's what I think about when Ambellina buckles into her strap-on and pushes me over the table, her thick hand around my neck closing my windpipe, the weight of her wide hips pressing against me. It hurts. "Poor Theo," she says, her nails tearing across my back. "My little Tolstoy. You just want to hide here." And I nod because when I don't nod the beatings will start again.

The fog is pouring over Twin Peaks into the Mission. It tumbles down the hillside, blanketing the small white houses. It was so warm the other day. When the fog pushes in, the valley gets cold. In Chicago the buildings are mountains but here the hills are real. The wind cuts down the streets. In a few hours the city will be grey. They're running elections for supervisor, and the streets are peppered with slogans. Ammiano for Tenants' Rights. Cheng for Change. Men are selling paperbacks next to Macondo and the Kilowatt. The cardboard placards fly down the street. I'm standing at a payphone next to the movie theater, across from the Copy King where I pick up my mail. It's five o'clock. People are stepping off and onto trains, getting home from work.

I hold my collar tight around my neck. "I can't meet you," Ambellina says. She does this. She cancels on me a lot. She wants to know what I'm wearing. She wants to talk sexy. "Get me off," she says. "Imagine me hitting you. Imagine the phone between my legs. I'm sitting on your face. I'm smothering you. You can't breathe."

"I'm on a payphone," I say. "People can see me."

"Are you ashamed?" she asks.

"Yes," I respond.

"That's your problem. Have Friday open for me."

"Bell, I can't."

"You what?"

"I have to work."

A bus has stopped in front of me and the driver is out in the street pulling frantically on the cables, his passengers staring through the windows, an old Chinese woman stuck at the rear door trying to get out.

"Do you know how many submissives answered my ad?" She waits for my answer. "Do you know how many men there are like you, who want a strong woman to keep them in place? Do you think you're the only one I could have? There's thousands of men like you. I get letters every day."

"I'm sorry."

"Do you think I care about that?" she asks. There's a long pause, like she's considering what to say next. "Listen. You will see me when I want to see you. You will make time for me when I tell you to. You will," she says. "You will." Then she hangs up on me. I place my fingers against my forehead and try to block out the sounds of the city, the shoes on the pavement and the sewers. I lean against the Currency Exchange, next to a street vendor selling old magazines, and sit down for a second on the sidewalk.

Valerie is running from the cauldrons to the toaster, a bright, pink flash of light. I close the lid on the pickle bucket and she shoves a square tub of peanut butter forward and I grab it before it smacks the side of the machine. "Back so soon?" she asks. One click, one shot. Two clicks. Bagels at the toaster. Jam. Cream cheese.

"I'm taking a cigarette break," Valerie says. She stands in the fire exit with a cigarette, looking back at the counter to make sure a line doesn't form. There's never been a fire here. Valerie is thirty-five and twice divorced. She dresses like a schoolgirl with her pink pigtails but the creases around her mouth and her eyes give her away. Her turquoise pantyhose, intentionally torn at the calf, stop before her skirt. We used to go to concerts together before Philc started coming around. Now she has one arm crossed over her chest holding her elbow. Philc has a small BMX bike as high as my knees and he is standing on the front wheel of it now, bouncing near the muffin boxes. "Check this out," he says to Valerie, swinging the little bicycle under his leg.

"That's so good, Philc."

* * *

I think I expressly said I was looking for a sub in my ad. If you are now my sub, then by definition I am your mistress. Please address me accordingly.

Forget about Friday if it is such a hassle. I shall see you in a few weeks.

Pat owns a string of bagel shops but this one was his first. They used to make the bagels next door but now that's a photo studio and the bagels are baked in a warehouse near Potrero Hill. The store was opened in the '60s, a gathering spot for protesters. We have a news article framed on the wall above the ATM and it's a picture of a young Pat on a stage speaking to an enormous crowd on a grass lawn with university buildings in the background. The headline reads "Students Say: Not Our War!"

He comes in while we're closing. He likes to tell us stories of San Francisco's past. "You used to get a lid of grass for twenty dollars. You could have sex with a thirteen- year- old girl and when her mom asked about it you did her too."

"I doubt it," Valerie says.

I lock the door for the night and Pat sparks a joint. I take a hit and hand it to Valerie. We're tired. We've been on our feet all day.

"Yeah, well. I exaggerate sometimes. Keeps life interesting." Pat folds his hands across his large stomach and lets out a sigh. Valerie's laugh is like birdsong. "I ought to start drug testing you guys. If it's OK with Clinton that makes it unanimous. Fucking Reagan. Here's your war on drugs." Pat takes a long smoke and leans his head back, smoke gurgling out between his lips and dribbling up his face. A fifty-year-old hippie in a tie-dyed shirt and blue jeans. He's probably worth a million bucks.

* * *

Report in immediately. I'm waiting.

At the Dress for Less I tell the saleslady I'm buying underwear for my girlfriend and she asks me what size my girlfriend is and I say, "Oh, she's about my size."

The apartment's never clean enough for Ambellina. I don't own very much but what I have lacks character. Just white space. I live on the third floor and dust seems to collect from the windows. I have new dust every day. She told me to prepare her something to eat so I bought chicken breasts and spinach at the Buy-rite and they're ready for her but she doesn't seem hungry. "Did you get any wine?" she asks. I pour her a glass of wine, hand it to her, kneel down in front of her. She smells thick, like milk and brown sugar. "Amuse me," she says. I look around my own apartment. There is nothing here. I have a small television on a short, dark stand. I have a Monopoly game, a table, a mattress, a small couch, a phone, an answering machine with blue buttons. I don't even know how I amuse myself. "Are you trying to manipulate me?" Ambellina asks. "Is this what I want or what you want?"

I flinch when Ambellina raises her hand. I close my eyes and wait. At Prairie View they said I had a twitch. Out in the woods by the border of Wisconsin with other bad children, miles from the nearest hitchhiking road, surrounded by brown trees, trunks as thick as truck tires. All the doors are locked and you have to ask permission just to use the bathroom. They run it on a point system. Henry Horner Children's Adolescent Center on the grounds of Reed Mental Hospital uses time-out rooms and drugged Kool-Aid and straps you to a bed when things get out of hand. Thorazine was big for kids in the '80s. They never let you speak in court. They keep log books full of your flaws. Pass notes about you back and forth, from social worker to case worker to therapist to hospital intern. They never let you read what they've written.

I want to tell Ambellina something, but I don't trust her. She squeezes the handcuffs closed on my wrists. She also has a blindfold, which she wraps over my eyes. She runs tape over my mouth and I start to shake my head no and scream but it's just muffled and she's telling me to shut up again but I can't. I knock into the wall. Bang my head against the wall. Everything inside of me is black and rushing forward, stopping in front of that big wad of tape. She pins me with her leg while she chains my ankles. I'm telling myself not to scream but as I struggle the handcuffs get tighter, cutting the circulation to my wrists. I keep screaming strange, muffled sounds into this tape. I can't control myself. My mouth fills with glue. And she's slapping me and then punching me. "Stop it," she says, reaching between my legs, squeezing hard, her other fist landing against my eye. "Stop it." It's like glass, like a car crash, like being held underwater.

I'm on the floor and Ambellina is on the mattress, my face between her legs when she rips the tape off my mouth. I feel the skin of her thighs. It feels warm and it feels like it is everywhere around me and I'm floating and breathing somehow in this dark pool. "Do you want me to take the blindfold off?" she asks and I whisper *no*. But it hardly comes out so I shake my head no and she touches my hair. I'm damp. I feel her body moving around me and the dark room. I feel safe. She says something about her child. A girl. She sounds sad but I can't make out what she's saying. Something about her husband and her child. She's very sad about something.

*   *   *

In the morning Valerie has a black eye and I do too. She's stacking plates. I heft a forty-pound sack of beans from beneath the counter. Somebody knocks on the door and then runs away. We're still closed. My body hurts and I feel like I will never get better.

"I don't want to talk about it," Valerie says. Valerie's black eye extends down her cheekbones where it becomes yellow.

It's seven o'clock. We're done setting up. Neither of us makes a move to open the door. A lady in black pants, a white shirt, and a blazer is knocking. Valerie stares at her but doesn't do anything. Valerie shouldn't worry. This is our café. I pull out a rag and rub down the display case. The lady knocks harder and pulls on the handle, *cack cack cack*, as the deadbolt rattles through the plate glass. "She doesn't need any coffee," I say. "She's already awake."

But Valerie goes to the door and lets the woman in. The woman has a tight face that pulls forward to the tip of her nose, her skin stretched over the hollows of her cheeks, her mouth small and circular. She looks from Valerie to me, sees our black eyes, and decides not to say anything more than "One large coffee please." She looks at her thin gold watch. "I'm late," she says helplessly.

The lady leaves but more people follow and Valerie and I run back and forth, turning the crank that keeps the shop operating. The junkies fill up the back room. We pour old espresso into the iced coffee jug, stack orange juice and mini-containers full of lox spread and white fish salad. Philc comes in at some point. He pushes the girl who is on the nod at the table near the dishbin. "Get up," he says. "You owe me a soup packet." She looks up from her arms, her face covered with tattoos. "I'll cut you," Philc says, sorting through her bags—a black garbage bag and a Barbie lunchbox.

"Theo."

A line of customers is forming in the front of the store. But I'm watching Philc and when he realizes I'm watching him and that Valerie is watching him he jumps up and spreads his arms in the middle of the floor.

"Ta-da!" he says. He does a dance step where he walks a perfect square. Then he tries to walk behind the counter but I stop him with the broom.

"You can't come back here. You don't work here."

"What are you doing?" he asks me, his face turning red, throwing his hand slightly forward and spreading his fingers, like he's letting go of something and that I should be wary.

"What are you doing?" Valerie asks.

"He doesn't belong behind the counter," I say to Valerie and her black eye and back to Philc, who is looking at the floor now and rummaging in his jacket pocket for the handle to something.

I poke Philc in the sternum with the broom.

"You think you could take me, bro?" Philc asks, turning his head ninety degrees into his shoulder, crunching his ear against his collarbone, then walking away from me, slapping a fist into his palm. He walks straight back to the emergency exit muttering, "You think you could take me?" Philc kicks open the emergency exit. It opens to a small yard filled with garbage and recycling.

"C'mon," Philc says, standing next to the bathroom door, biting at his lips.

"Get out of here," I say.

"You're not part of this," he tells me. He raises his boot and lowers it as hard as he can onto the foot of the girl with the tattooed face and she wakes with a loud scream and falls to the floor holding her foot. Philc pulls a rock out, whips it past my shoulder, and a bottle of syrup breaks. He runs up and puts a foot into the glass display case.

"You don't belong here," I say.

"You don't belong here," he answers me back as the front door closes behind him. The girl in the back has curled into a ball and is making small, high-pitched noises. Glass and syrup are everywhere. It's just glass and syrup but I don't know what to do about it.

I look over at Valerie and she's crying so hard she's choking. She looks like a mermaid, her pink hair, all those tears.

We've closed up. Pat is coming to look at the damage. Pat knows, with all of his talk of revolution, this is junkie central. The cost of doing business. I'm cleaning up the glass and mopping the syrup. There's glass in the bagels so I throw all of the bagels away. Valerie straightens the countertop, dumps out the coffee that's getting old and starting to burn, fastens the cap on the container of purple onions sliced from this morning. Picks up the pastries and throws them away.

"That's where you get that black eye," Valerie says. "You like to fight. You like to pick fights. You like to pick fights with people's boyfriends." She's still puffy-faced and red.

"No," I say. "That's not how I got this."

"Fuck you, Theo," she says. "Fuck you and your problems."

I'm wearing women's underwear and leather pants at the 16th Street BART station, worried that someone will see me when Ambellina gets off the train. We walk back three blocks to my apartment, past the liquor stores and the transient hotels. Men with blankets on their shoulders huddle between doorways next to the Quick Mart. "You should have gotten me a cab," she says. There's been a fire in the red building on Van Ness. It's a single-room occupancy, and spray-painted on the brick is

Death to landlords. "I'm in marriage counseling. You didn't know that." Ambellina pulls out a cigarette. She never smoked before. She shakes her head. I almost tell her that I was married once. How I got thrown out of the abortion clinic downtown. But I think better of it, because she'd want to know why, or she wouldn't want to know at all. And anyway years have passed, and this is today. "I have a daughter," she says. She hands me her lighter and when I light her cigarette for her she blows the smoke in my face. "Yesterday, in front of our counselor, I told my husband I was leaving him." She stops and I stop with her. She doesn't even seem to care that I almost kept walking. "What do you think will happen to my little girl? Answer," she says. We're in front of my building.

"We should go inside," I suggest.

"You can do better than that."

"Bell, I don't know anything about children."

"Open this damn door," she says.

I make her a cup of coffee. She stands by the window peering cautiously through the blinds to the street. I crawl to her on my knees. She looks down at me skeptically. "You couldn't give me what I want in a million years," she says. She places her leg on a chair and guides my face to her and tells me where to lick and where to suck. "That's where my husband fucks me," she says. I'm stretching my neck as she lifts beneath my chin, surrounded by her legs. "Stop," she says, pushing me away. Stripping her top and skirt. She's getting fat. "Do you think I'm the most beautiful woman?"

"I do," I say. We're going through the motions. The next forty minutes is spent with me trying to please her with my tongue until my mouth is dry and sore.

She slaps me a few times over by the couch and for a moment I think this is going to work. She hits me particularly hard once and I feel my eye starting to swell again and she stops. "Lie down on the bed," she says. "My husband doesn't want me to do this." She slides over me. Of course I'm not wearing protection. Nothing is safe. She rides up over me. Like an oven. She says, "Theo, darling." She grabs my hands and places them on her thighs. She lies on top of me, biting me lightly. I grip her legs and stay quiet. Her chest against my chest. This is sex. There's no real threat. If I yell loud enough she'll stop, which leaves us with nothing. And when I say I exist only to please her I don't mean it. And when she tells me how beautiful she is it's because she doesn't believe it. Or when she says she has to punish me and asks me if I'm scared, she doesn't mean it. We don't mean it.

Ambellina is wrapping a belt around her skirt. I turn away from her and watch the door. "My husband would like to see me with you. He wants to see me with a submissive. Then he'll realize it's not a threat to him. Because, of course you are not. Then, when I'm done with you, he'll make love to me like a real man. We'll discuss it first. I want you to come over to the East Bay."

I walk her down the stairs, past the bicycles locked to the stairwell and onto the Mission streets. Ambellina gets in the cab and I give the driver my money. "Take her to Oakland," I tell him. "She has to meet her husband."

"I'll see you on Tuesday," Ambellina says.

"I love you," I tell her back.

Pat and I meet at the Uptown on 17th Street. A holdover from the revolution. The walls are covered with slogans for left-wing political movements. The tables are carved and stickered. There are two red couches in the back, a jukebox and a pool table, a view of the hookers who walk by at street level. Pat orders us two Speakeasys and two shots of whiskey and he pays for them. He always pays for the drinks and we never talk about it. He starts like he always does. "In the sixties," he says, drinking his beer, "we were trying to change society."

"So much for that idea," I tell him.

"You'd be amazed how much fun you can have if you get out of your own head. The problem is that now people are only interested in themselves. What we have is a non-voting generation. That's what they should call you guys, the non-voting generation. You think you can't fix anything until you fix yourselves. Well, let me be the first to tell you, you will never fix yourself."

Somebody throws some money into the jukebox at the same time a rack of pool balls slams into the gully. The Pixies, *I will grow, up to be, be a debaser.*

"My wife," I tell Pat. "I didn't always sell bagels."

"What about your wife?"

"Oh man. She was a sweetheart. Long legs, black hair. When people met her they said she had breeding. Because she walked so straight. But you know, she didn't. I mean, we didn't always get along. Like, we didn't agree on a lot of things. We hated each other. She wanted things from me. I felt like I could never give them to her."

Pat's looking in his whiskey glass with one eye waiting for me to finish. I know all about Pat's marriage. His childhood girlfriend. And how her head isn't right anymore. "So what's wrong with selling bagels?"

"Nothing wrong with it." I drink my beer. Pat's good for at least one more round. Maybe two. A perk of the job, I suppose, but still, I'm the one that has to be up at six in the morning. I only live two blocks away from this bar. I come here when the phone is ringing. I sit here at night with a beer, not trying to get drunk, just trying to make it last. I like to watch the young couples that come in here and sit next to each other on the couch.

I love it when they lean into one another even though the couch is long, cutting off their own space.

"Listen," Pat says. "There's a whole world out there. How old are you?"

"Thirty-three."

"Keep going, man. You'll be full manager. What would you do if you were the manager right now? If I said, Theo, you are now the manager of Hoff Bagels. I'm talking profit sharing. The whole business. What would you do?"

I look at Pat slyly. "I'd change the world," I tell him, putting down my beer. "If I was manager there'd be no more war."

Pat looks at me for a second like he's going to laugh, but then he gets the joke and a queer expression passes over his face. It's like somebody's taken the air out of him. He sips on the bottom of his whiskey shot and then chases it with his beer. I give him a blank stare. "Yeah, well," he says, and I feel guilty already. "No need to worry about that. Have another one, all right?"

"All right," I say.

I send Ambellina a note that I won't be able to see her any more, then sign off the kiosk and go to help Valerie behind the counter. I don't know why I have to end it with Ambellina. Because nothing in my life has ever worked out quite the way I planned. Because I'm selfish. I do it because I'm lonely and when I don't see her it's worse and because after three years in San Francisco I don't know anybody. Because I don't want to be seen and I don't want anybody to know. Because she was so human the last time I saw her, unsure of her next move. And I don't have room for that, for reasons I'm unsure of. My small apartment. This city and all of the cities. No. And the jungles with their animals. People with their problems. The windows. I woke last night and grabbed at the end of my mattress. The windows. No. It's hard enough.

Valerie doesn't want to talk to me. One time Valerie asked me to walk her to the campsite. She said she was afraid to go alone. All of the homeless were there, below the highway, at the base of Bernal Heights. Shopping carts were everywhere and they had strung tarp among them. A large fire was burning from a steel drum and we saw the men and women huddled around it from across Cesar Chavez. I asked Valerie why she wanted to go there though I knew it was to see Philc. But I didn't understand that she had to go down beneath the highway and the thick traffic, a six-lane-deep river to be crossed. It looked like hell to me, that place she was going to, all the people and stray dogs. Valerie looked at me like she didn't know what I meant. "I'm not going there," I told her. Valerie crossed her arms. "You don't have to go there," I said. She thought about it but then she stepped into the street, wading through the traffic and I watched for a minute and then followed. We climbed out the other side and nobody seemed to care who we were. We found Philc's tent near the back, where everybody threw away their trash. Paper and soiled, torn clothing was everywhere, piles stacked against the steel mesh fence before the brickyard. He was standing, throwing a knife into the dirt. There were a couple of men sitting nearby sipping on the last of a glass bottle and wiping their beards. One of the men had a bag of peeled carrots on his lap.

"Is that your bodyguard?" Philc sneered. Valerie left me and went over to him. "I've been doing speed. Watch this." He pushed Valerie over to a big tree. She seemed to know what to do. She leaned back against it with her arms straight at her sides and closed her eyes. She looked happy. "Are you guys watching?" he asked the two men. One of them nodded and the other grabbed a carrot stub from his bag. Philc picked up his knife. A truck rumbled over the steel girders, sending a shiver through the small plot. Philc threw the knife, striking the tree right next to Valerie's head. But it didn't stick. It fell to the ground and landed bent at her feet.

"That's dangerous," I said.

"Fuck," Philc said, gathering his knife. Valerie had opened her eyes.

"Let's go," I told her.

"She's not going anywhere," Philc said, looking down at his knife, running his fingers along the blade like he was cleaning it.

"You go," Valerie said. "I'll be okay."

"She's safe with me." Philc's dirty face was full of challenge. "There's room for her in my tent." He emptied a bottle of water onto a rag. There didn't seem to be anything for me to do but to go. I wasn't wanted and it was obvious Valerie wasn't leaving unless I carried her out, and I wasn't going to do that. I didn't want to watch Philc throw knives at her head. I worked my way down the path and lowered myself back into the street.

It's game night. The tables are filled with people playing board games. Twenty people, maybe. This group comes here once a week. I don't know who they are. They show up. They order some coffee. We stay open later than usual. They set up Monopoly, checkers, parcheesi. Push the pieces. They play for hours.

"This is our strangest night," I say to Valerie. But she's still upset so she doesn't even answer. "Valerie, look at them," I say over her shoulder. She's wearing a Naked Raygun shirt. *Last Tour Ever*. She's cutting a bagel for a customer. She ignores me. "I don't even know what I want. If somebody asked me what I wanted I couldn't even begin to answer them."

"But nobody's asking, are they?" Valerie says.

"No," I say. She's facing me with the knife. Somebody shouts *Yahtzee!* Valerie's lips, at the corners, point down. "Nobody is."

I clean up my apartment. It doesn't take long, it's such a small place. I knock on my neighbor's door and ask if I can borrow his broom and I sweep my floors. I fill a bucket with soap and water and wash the walls. I leave my hands in the dark, soapy water for a minute. I stand by the window and watch the action on the street below, the hookers and the police cruisers. If I was in Chicago with my wife, we'd watch television. We'd avoid the obvious questions. We'd make excuses for nothing until we were done and we could finally sleep. Then the phone starts ringing.

I buy Valerie a five-dollar bar of soap that smells like cucumber. I take out the trash. Lunchtime, Philc is standing across Valencia Street. He has scratches on his cheek and a new tattoo under his eye. I pass him on my way to pick up pizza slices for Valerie and myself. We look at each other but I just keep walking. It's three in the afternoon and the shop is empty except for the girl with the tattooed face who's on the nod at the last table in the back.

I remember when that girl started coming around the neighborhood, with her Barbie lunchbox, looking to get high. People would say she was pretty, except for the tattoos. It's like she only had that one thing wrong with her, but that was enough. The blue ink obscures her face entirely. It runs from her ears and eyes and curls under her chin like a beard. She gets in cars and turns tricks down by Folsom Street.

Valerie has finished her slice and is throwing away the paper plate. She pours herself a soda and dumps three ounces of peach syrup into it. She wipes her mouth with her forearm and then puckers her lips.

The light is blinking on the machine and all of my windows are open. The workers from the factory are huddled around the white lunch truck.

You fucking punk bitch. You think you can send me an email saying you don't want to see me anymore and that's it? I don't know what kind of game you are playing. Be as close to a man as you can be and pick up the motherfucking phone or do something that makes me less inclined to rip your fucking thinning hair out by the pale roots. I really don't have time for your shit. You belong on your back with me suffocating you. Why do you think there is room for you? Don't you think I have my own problems? I will ambush you somewhere. I will leave permanent marks. I warn you, don't fuck with me. You can't run away. I will be there tomorrow and if you are not available your whole neighborhood will know what a sissy punk bitch who likes to be raped you are. Don't underestimate my cruelty.

At work I stand near the counter. "C'mon," Valerie says. I take a breath before wrapping the last bagel of the morning in paper and handing it to the customer who walks out the door. Outside they're routing traffic around Valencia and the cars, each pointing in a slightly different direction, seem to be trying to climb over one another but none of them are moving. The cars need to get through. There is no way around Valencia. It's starting to rain. People run past the windows with papers over their hats. Philc and Valerie are in the back with the recycling and the trash, having a cigarette under the porch hang. I open the newspaper; there's been an invasion. I look up and Philc is standing at the counter in front of me. "Hey," he says quietly. "We need to come to an understanding, bro." I fold the newspaper, slide it over by the cookies. "Valerie loves you. Do you know that, man? You're family. You are. I think we can make this work." He pulls a toothpick from his pocket and plays with it between his front teeth. "Maybe we can all get a place together. You know what I mean? The three of us. No more bad times." He speaks calmly and I wonder what kind of pills he's been taking and if they would do me any good and how long they would last. "Friends for life?" He stretches his hand across the counter. I take his hand because every small bit of peace is worth having.

I put the bagels away and wrap the day-old pastries. Valerie comes back to help me. The rain is beating down on the sidewalk and Philc is sitting quietly in the back making origami from napkins.

That time you were tied up before. You looked so innocent. I wanted to draw blood. But I didn't. Do you know why? You like to think you're smart so you think other people can't understand you. You are so funny! Did you ever think I was reasonable? I mean, I can be a reasonable person but I don't like being played with. You cannot spend time with me and then send some pathetic excuse to disappear. Is that how you handle things? By running away? It doesn't work like that little boy. Answer your phone next time I call.

I tell Ambellina I'm sorry and ask if I can take her to see *Casablanca* at the Paramount in Oakland. It's been raining every day and I head to the East Bay. The Paramount is an art deco theater from the Depression that plays classic movies. The theater opens early for cocktails and the Wurlitzer. I'm there first, above the Nineteenth Street station, and after fifteen minutes I start to worry that she isn't going to show up and then she is standing in front of me. I try to take her hand but she won't let me. "What do you think you were trying to pull?" she asks. We're moving with the crowd of people down the street.

"I..."

"You what? Do you belong to me or not?" Men are watching her. She's wearing thigh-high latex yellow boots, fishnets, a leather skirt. Her tight curls are cut close to her scalp and dyed arctic blue. She seems to be looking around, smiling to all of them at once. She also seems to be focused only on me.

"Yes," I say quietly.

"What?"

"Yes. I belong to you, Mistress." The guy walking next to me snickers.

We move through the large doors of the old theater, the velvet floors, columns and statues reaching to a roof that ends in a midnight sky. The theater was built to hold thousands. Ambellina sends me for Coke and popcorn and when I come back the seats around us are filled and the man in the coat and tails at the Wurlitzer is being lowered beneath the stage.

Bogart's face fills the screen and out of the corner of my eye Ambellina is rummaging through her purse. I grew up with Humphrey Bogart. We had a television and my father loved the old Bogart films and would make me watch them. *Casablanca, The Maltese Falcon, Key Largo.* "You're not big enough to take me down, see." In his better moods my father would quote Bogart. "Sure, on the one hand maybe I love you and maybe you love me. But you'll have something on me you can use whenever you want. And since I'll have something on you who's to say you're not going to knock me over like you did the rest of them?" My father was a big man with a loud laugh, four inches taller than I am now. He was a violent man who wouldn't stand for being looked at crossways by women or children. He pushed my kindergarten teacher down a small flight of stairs. He carried a small gun, a bottle of mace, and brass knuckles inside his coat. He was lazy and his laziness made him a criminal. He was killed with a shotgun just before my eleventh birthday, which is when my hard time began, though it might have already been too late.

Bogart seems friendly to me, among the roulette wheels and the card tables. His confidence. His big sad eyes. The white linen suits moving casually across the screen while the world is at war all around them. Rick's, a little Free French outpost on the sand. He does what he has to. He betrays poor Peter Lorre to the Nazis. But the world won't let him alone. The world is bigger than the castle he has built for himself. This is the lesson of *Casablanca*.

Ambellina forces the gag into my mouth and I catch my breath. I let out a tiny moan while the big, round puck forces open my jaw and cheeks, sending a throbbing up the sides of my face.

"Shhh."

The theater is so quiet except for the actors and Ambellina slowly rubbing her thumb and index finger together. There's a hole in the puck to breathe through and I feel her pulling the straps around the back of my neck and fastening it tight to hold the gag in. I grip onto the seats. The strap catches and pulls my hair. I want to move out of this. To squirm. To wriggle down to the floor. I jerk my head one way, and then back. One quick breath. I push back in my seat, my feet pressing the floor. I try to hold the middle and when I can't I lean cautiously into Ambellina's shoulder, and she lets me stay there. Before the plane flies away I've grown used to the pressure against the roof of my mouth. When the lights come on I'm resting; I can hardly feel my hair caught in the buckle.

"C'mon now, Angel," Ambellina says, unfastening the gag, sliding her fingers inside my cheeks to pull the puck from my mouth. "I'm taking you home."

CHAPTER THREE

ACHTERBURGWAL

I'M DREAMING OF my wife. I'm remembering her when she was pregnant, and then when she wasn't pregnant anymore. She was long and thin again after her pregnancy and I could fall asleep with her on top of me. She was so light I could barely feel her.

I scratch at my shoulder blades as I wake up and hear water boiling over a pot and spilling into a fire. The cotton sheet rides to my knees. I remember that I'm in Amsterdam and I haven't seen my wife Zahava in years. There's a woman in front of me at an ironing board wearing socks that don't reach her ankles, her legs naked until her shirt begins at her thighs. She's looking down on me. Her white T-shirt is so bright it appears out of focus. I wonder if she is going to hit me with the iron.

"I don't know you," I say.

"You will," she says. She stands the iron on its heels. Her calves stretching, she jerks the plug from the wall.

Her name is Jessie and she's a friend of my roommate Toine, who has left for work already. Toine and I share a small flat in the Jordan: two rooms with no doors, the shower hanging over the toilet, the kitchen the length and width of a plank.

There's a packet of croissants between Jessie and me with the plastic ripped open. We lean against the counters and eat from plates we hold with one hand. She's taller than me but not as tall as Toine. She's beautiful, I think, though I didn't notice it right away. She's big-boned, like the Dutch, but with black hair, and her skin is the color of sand.

"Toine and I met in college," Jessie says. "I don't suppose he ever mentioned me?"

"We've only lived together for a couple of months," I say. She watches me eating and I cover my mouth. "He's moving soon. He never mentioned you."

"Of course not. Why would he? You're just roommates, right?" She lays her plate on the counter, next to the wood block and the knives. "But we were very close. He wanted to marry me, except that we were political. Can you imagine Toine at a protest?"

"No." I place my plate in the sink and brush my hands together. "I have to go to work." I squeeze between Jessie and the fridge to grip the tap, run a stream of water over my plate and pull the pan she cooked eggs in from the stove, wipe it twice with a rag and hang it on the wall. Jessie hasn't moved; she's waiting for something and I frown and smile at the same time to show her I'm in a hurry.

"You don't have to look at me like that. I have work to do as well. I'm not some crazy person, you know. I'm not a stalker."

"I never said you were a stalker."

"I've just returned from Africa," she tells me. "Ever been? I was doing very important work there. There's a report I have to write. Tell Toine I'll still be here when he gets home."

* * *

It's a damp Dutch day and the bricks in the street are wet. The tourists haven't woken yet but the laundries are open and some of the hookers have turned on the lights in their windows. Toine is across from the fountain before the theater Casa Rosso, standing in front of the kiosk. He wears his dark blue suit and tie, his toes pointed toward the short rail that borders the canal. He seems to be considering what to do about the water.

"Up early," I say, shoving my hands in my pockets and spitting at the canal.

"Up Simba," he says and flips his cigarette into the canal. He looks the way he always looks, happy, disgusted, bored. "I was restless. I thought I'd leave you Jessie."

"What's wrong with her?" I say. "There's something wrong with her."

"She doesn't know when she isn't wanted. You would make a nice couple."

"She's beautiful," I say.

"I'll tell you something about beauty. She left Holland years ago to save the world. She thought she would spread a curtain and wrap the hungry children in it and they wouldn't be hungry anymore. Now she comes back because I have a career. She arrived last night with her bags while you were sleeping. Can you imagine?" He shakes his head. He takes a flat pad of tickets from inside the empty ticket booth and hands them to me, then reaches into his pocket for some coins. "Have you had coffee?"

"No."

"Here's three gulden. Get two cups from Harry."

Where I work it looks like a theater, a smaller version of where Toine stands, but it isn't. There are pictures from the actual show cased in glass along the outside: Hank and Melinda fucking on a trapeze, Miriam sticking a banana in her pussy, Lucy smoking a cigar with her vagina, the lesbians. The stairs are carpeted and lead to a small landing with a podium where I write my tickets in front of a wall full of mirrors and what looks like a door with a golden handle. But it's all an illusion. The door opens to a storage closet where costumes are kept. There's no show here. This is just a rented storefront. The show is down the street, where the windows cost more, where it's so crowded on the weekends your shoulders get stuck. But some people come in this way.

"Live sex show," I call out. "See Mickey's mouse." I sell a couple of tickets before noon. I write out a card on the podium and initial my name at the bottom of it next to the price they paid. I make eight percent on each ticket plus the first sixty gulden. I can charge between fifteen and fifty gulden. The customers wait in front of the golden handle to the storage closet for me to open the door for them. "It's not there," I say, tucking the ticket pad into my pocket. "Follow me."

"Where are you going?" an American in a rugby shirt asks, reaching for my collar. "Give me my money back."

I avoid his hand. "I'm taking you to the theater."

"I thought this was the theater."

"You'll be happy when you see it." I try to walk quickly to stay ahead of them, but not so quick they panic. "You see," I say, arriving at the Casa Rosso, pointing toward the facade. "It's not a fake."

"You're a fake," the man says. "You're a fucking clown."

"You can go in now," Toine says. He takes their tickets and folds the slips into his pile, then opens the door for them. "You're having a day," he says to me. "Good for you."

"OK. Two hundred gulden. How about you?"

"Sometimes more, sometimes less." He takes his cigarette from his mouth and turns his hands over so the cigarette disappears. He turns his hands back and the cigarette is still gone, but his hands are both smoking. He smiles at me and the cigarette slides from between his lips, the smoke channeling along his cheeks. Then I walk back to my spot and try again.

After leaving Chicago, I traveled for almost two years before I wound up here. My wife had been staying with her lover in his condominium. I offered to move in with them and stay in the other room and she looked at me like I was some kind of monster, but I was the one looking for a solution. "I mean it," I said. "You won't even know I'm there."

She walked away. It was too much for me, the apartment without her. I didn't mean to end up in Amsterdam. But this is where I ran out of money and found a job.

I don't work often at night, which is when the Banana Bar opens and the barkers make most of their money. It's after seven now and I'm drinking and watching Adel, the Nigerian prostitute. She rents the most expensive window in the red light district, just around the corner from the main theater. It's getting dark and the streetlamps are coming on along with the fluorescent bars along the top of the windows. The streets are pink.

Toine works the evening shift and I hear him calling tourists. Through the mist I can make out the edge of the neon sign pointing north. I watch Adel from a safe distance near the New Bridge. Toine sleeps with her sometimes and tells me she doesn't charge him.

This is where I spend my evenings. A student is playing guitar on the bridge. The student's friend dances on his heels, like something out of a children's book, and waves a fedora around for change. The pickpockets are looking for customers. The Nigerian pushes herself up on her toes. I lean against the pylon as the streets swell. The owner of the bar on the far end of the district comes floating past with his dog at the wheel of his short barge.

I should go but I stay here where it's light and noisy, the air filled with reefer, urine, and perfume. Hypodermics and trash float against the canal walls. Toine's friend Jessie is home alone, probably setting our apartment on fire. Behind us, a man painted green is stripped to the waist and juggling bowling balls as if they were balloons. Toine's baritone hovers over all of it like an umbrella. "Step right up, young lovers. You're not here for the architecture. Ladies and gentlemen, step right up."

Late, when the last show has already begun, I return to the theater. Yuen holds the door open for me, parting his gold teeth, holding his suitcase with his other hand. I climb the red carpets into the balcony where the bar is. Jessie stands with Toine. She's changed into a flowered shirt and white slacks that hug her waist and she looks transformed from this morning and innocent among the salesmen here, all of whom wear dark suits. "I hope you got a discount," I tell her and she laughs. She touches my shoulder.

"Someone's been drinking already," Jessie says.

Taco is bartending. A necklace of coconut halves is strung over the entrance to the dressing room. Miriam in her grass skirt is saying something quiet and urgent to Rynant the bouncer.

"Where did you go?" Toine asks. "I thought you would keep Jessie company after you got off, but you never went home."

"He doesn't like me," Jessie says. "He's afraid of girls."

"That's ridiculous," I say. "I tied one on."

"Allow yourself to be teased," Jessie says. "You'll enjoy life more."

"Don't lecture people," Toine tells her. "They don't like it."

Jessie makes a pouty face and pinches Toine's elbow.

"She's dangerous," he jokes, leaning forward so the bar lights crawl under his chin. "Imagine, coming back to me after so many years. What could be more corrupt?"

"Beer, Theo?" Taco asks.

"Yes. And one for my friends."

Miriam emerges on the stage below us, wearing a cape, dancing to Surinamese drum rhythms, and Hank scrambles out behind the curtain in the gorilla outfit. She's painted WAR in bright green letters across her stomach. She steps from her skirt and jumps into the crowd, her long red cape flashing behind her, her bare feet smacking the armrests. She climbs along the customers on the first floor. She wraps her cape around a woman's head. When Miriam pulls the cape back, her underwear is gone, her pubic hair inches from the woman's nose. She scoots closer, bringing the woman's face between her legs. Hank looks puzzled, scratches his head, then begins to play with himself, spraying the crowd with water from the plastic gorilla penis. When it's over Miriam pulls Hank from the stage by a chain.

The lesbian show is starting. Victoria ambles forward in her police outfit with her thumbs tucked in her pockets and her hat cocked. Alexis waits for her in a shimmering metal dress, clutching the stage pole in her hands. Victoria told me one night that there are too many foreigners here. "No offense," she said. "I mean the Arabs." And the Arabs are in the front now for her show. Sheiks with magnificent turbans of all colors bundled over their heads. Yuen and Toine will always approach the Arabs and ask if they need women because the rich Arabs are too discreet to visit the girls who stand in the windows. Once a Pakistani general came dressed in full uniform and Toine sat with him and they talked about driving tanks through the Khyber Pass. Another time Toine sat in front with a small, hairless, pink man who wore only one long bolt of fabric like a toga. Toine later told me the man was the leader of a religion a million strong and there was a price on his head large enough to retire on. I thought he was encouraging me to kill the man and I got sick.

"I've never seen a sex show," Jessie says, placing her elbows behind her on the bar. Victoria has cuffed Alexis's wrists together and is inserting her baton into Alexis's vagina. "Do you think they enjoy it?"

"What's not to enjoy?" Toine asks.

Victoria rubs a teaspoonful of grease into Alexis's anus and slips her thumb inside. An artificial moan comes through the speakers. "We've had his presidents in here," Toine says, pointing at me. He finishes his beer and places the empty glass back on the bar near the spigots. "I'm so bored with this I could die."

Toine's room is in the front, where four windows overlook a quiet Dutch street. Not far from here is the Anne Frank Huis, but it doesn't look different from any of the others except for the sign.

"Tell me about America," Jessie says.

"America is a prison," I say.

Jessie balances a box of photographs on her knee as if it were a child. She runs a finger along her gumline. "You know, since last I saw you, I've been working in a refugee camp in the Congo. I worked there for three years."

"I know what you've been doing," Toine says, without looking up, tossing waves of cocaine with his blade.

"Mmmm. The Hutus used the camp as a base for killing missions into Rwanda until Médicins Sans Frontieres protested. The whole world ignored it," she says, stretching her arms high over her head. The box nearly falls, and she catches it. "So how did you come to live together?"

"This one? He's an orphan. I took him in."

"Is that true, Theo? Are you an orphan from an American prison?"

"I'm too old to be an orphan. I'm old enough to be a father."

"She cares about everybody," Toine says. It sounds as if he's apologizing for her.

"You sound bitter," Jesse says, smiling. "Anyway, I left Holland to go to Oxford and then took a job with the relief agency."

"You won't get what you came here for," Toine tells her, wagging a finger in her direction and then returning to his task. "You might as well go back to your refugee camps."

Jessie's leg is shaking. "You wouldn't believe the things you see. Have you heard of blue baby syndrome? In Gaza the water's poison and babies are born unable to breathe. The UN sets up another tank of water every time the Israelis bulldoze a building."

"She would clean the wells with a toothbrush so the Palestinians can have more babies," Toine says to me, then turns to Jessie. "Yuen is giving me the apartment behind the theater. Theo stays with me until I leave. I don't like living with people anymore."

"But it was nice of you to let Theo stay," she says. "So you're either not as mean as you pretend. Or you have something else planned."

"It was nice," I say, swallowing. The back of my throat is numb and hard. I pull on my forehead and try to stretch the skin. "Toine's the nicest person I've ever met."

I watch him use the razor like a chef, quickly splitting then crushing the piles together. Everything comes easy to him. He has the best spot. He outsells all of the other salesmen. He's Yuen's favorite. All of the women love him. He doesn't care about anything. The world gives him whatever he wants.

"Anyway," he says. "You haven't heard my story." I know what he's going to tell her. It's the first thing he told me when we first went for a drink. He had said I didn't look like I could work for the Casa Rosso because the district is such a violent place, but he went to Yuen and I was hired, because, he said, the space wasn't being used anyway. Our first night together he told me about the desert.

"Listen," Toine says to Jessie. "After you left to wash shit from the legs of black babies I bought a motorcycle. You don't know the difference between a two-stroke and a four-stroke bike, but what I had was a two-stroke. On a two-stroke bike you have to mix oil with the gasoline. It's meant for driving in places where there are no roads." Toine hands me the mirror to do my line first. This is also Toine's way. He knows he will always be left the longest line; he doesn't worry about it. He never shares a joint, he rolls everybody their own so he doesn't have to bother passing. "I took a boat to Algiers and rode into the Sahara. After fifteen days I was stopped by a caravan. Saharawi bandits still fighting for the Western Sahara with the Moroccans, the Spanish, and the French. That all ended without any result in 1991. But this was 1986. They took my motorcycle and left me in the dunes to die."

I snort my line and hand the mirror to Jessie, who places it over the box filled with photos. She's holding her leg steady and I'm worried she's going to start shaking again and send the last of the powder to the air.

"What happened?" she asks.

"The desert is growing," he says.

"I know that," she says.

"You don't know anything. These people are fighting over sand."

"I've seen more wars than you."

"Congratulations, G.I. Jane," he tells her dryly. "In El Oued they shovel it from their doorsteps in the mornings. The dunes have buried whole cities. It's like fighting the sea. Only the bandits know the Sahara. After three days, when the leaders of the bandits came in a car and drove me to an oasis, I didn't ask them any questions."

Jessie is leaning back with her arms at her sides. When I look at her now she looks a bit like my ex-wife, a little taller, a little prettier. Zahava also had black hair and liked cocaine. There was a time when my wife would do anything for some cocaine. If Zahava could see me now she wouldn't believe it. She always complained I lacked ambition.

I run my hand under my nose. Toine and Jessie's eyes are locked together. I bite at the inside of my mouth. I suspect the drugs don't affect him at all. He just likes to get other people high.

"It was thrilling, really," he says.

Jessie shakes her head then dives into the mirror. "We're only talking about ourselves," she says, lifting her face, snorting heavily, running her hands over her head as if she's just stepped from a pool. She sucks on her finger then picks up the mirror and hands it to Toine with both hands. "What's the most exciting thing you've ever done, Theo?"

"Hang out with you guys," I say, and they both laugh.

"You see why I let him stay."

"I like you," Jessie says. "You're nice."

At night I sleep with my memories and my Italian poster that Toine translated for me. I hear them arguing in the other room. They sound as if they're in the bed next to me. I squeeze my eyes shut, then open them.

"Please," she whispers.

"Be quiet," Toine says in a low, selfish voice.

I imagine Adel, the Nigerian prostitute, hitting me across my face with a whip, cutting my ear. I shake my head. I imagine Toine pulling me down the stairs by my hair. I concentrate, try to make my mind clear. My savings are gone now and I have what I make at the theater. My life before now wasn't worth anything.

I hear Toine's hand sliding over her body. I hear Jessie's low cry. I hear Toine say, "I won't."

I could sneak in the doorframe and watch them. I could crawl along the baseboard. If I could love I would have loved by now. To be in love, and want only the best for that person. My wife, Zahava, was always so happy. She never worried. When things stopped working, she spent time with a first-year lawyer named Mickey who had wide shoulders and thick black hair. It was his baby she got rid of.

"She's going to have to leave," Toine says. It's the afternoon already and we're near the Oude Kirk having dinner. It's been raining. The window is open and a priest is sitting with a table full of papers. He's not unfamiliar. There's a line of homeless waiting for the church to give them soup. The Oude Kirk is surrounded by prostitutes, some of them men, who cannot afford the more expensive windows near the Bulldog or the Achterburgwal. It's Toine's favorite place. Where the old meets the new, he says. Just behind the church is a public restroom, a tin cubicle that hides you from the street and a hole in the ground with a pipe that pours straight into the canal. It's Monday, the slowest day.

"What's wrong?" I ask. "She's pretty and smart. She loves you."

"She's half Asian and I'm Dutch," he says by way of explanation. I look at his cheeks to see if he is alluding to something else but his face doesn't give anything away. A door opens and a large man steps onto the cobblestone, his hair slicked across his head and his shirt tucked in. The prostitute he just visited stands behind him in the doorway, waiting for him to leave. The large man smiles benevolently and makes a big show of kissing the lady he's just paid. She nods then closes the door and pulls the curtain across it. She takes her place in front of the window.

"That's bullshit," I say and he shrugs. "That doesn't mean anything that she's Asian."

"Tell that to the Japanese. Say it doesn't mean anything that you are Japanese. Tell the Spanish their nationality is irrelevant, a genetic accident. You're still married, aren't you?" Toine asks. "You left your ring somewhere."

"I gave it away at the Taj Mahal, in Atlantic City."

"Good. I'm glad to hear you're a gambler. I have a wager for you."

"I'm not a gambler."

"But you come from gamblers."

"My father and my grandfather. But not my mother."

"You watch that black prostitute Adel. What is it about her? Why don't you ask her to marry you? She can finish a customer in less than ten minutes. That's six fucks an hour. You're lucky she doesn't have a pimp. She asks me why I let you stand there in front of her window every night. She says you scare away customers, and I tell her I am not your brother or your keeper." Toine's watching me and I'm staring back at him. "Forget it," he says. "I'll leave. You and Jessie can stay together. That's best."

"I don't want Jessie," I say.

"Why don't you tell me what you want?" Toine waits expectantly. I start to say something, but it gets caught between my ears and my mouth. I grab the table. Toine leans his head back and laughs. "Stay in Amsterdam as long as you want," he says. "It suits you. Look at the old priest. In the middle of all these whores and all he hears is pissing."

The streets are quiet now, only a few puddles of light from windows still open for business. Two street performers lie sleeping in jesters' hats, curled around the rail at the end of the bridge. Between the district and where we live there are four waterways and a set of tracks from the Terminus. I pass the new district where the new hostels are and the cafés are named for rock and roll bands—Café The Doors, Café Pink Floyd, where the tourists are still sitting on the porch quietly smoking marijuana. I've read that half the population of Amsterdam are illegal aliens.

At home I hang my jacket in the closet. My shirt is out. I pull my belt from my pants. "I've been waiting for you," Jessie says as I'm closing the closet door. She's standing in the small kitchen, smiling calmly, her makeup washed across her face from different directions. The knives are out and arranged by order of size along the cutting board. She hands me a beer already opened and I take it from her. She's only wearing a long cotton shirt again, like when I first saw her; it goes halfway to her knees.

There's a goblet full of red wine in the sink and she lifts it to her lips. Toine is not home. I take a sip from my beer. "Thank you."

"I'm going to leave," she says. "Because, you know what, some people can't be saved."

"I'm glad you're leaving." I turn on the light switch so we can see each other better. "It's the right thing to do. You're just hurting yourself."

She places her hand on the stove burner. "Just like you."

"I was married," I tell her.

"What did Toine do to you?" With a small movement she is only inches from me.

I hold my beer in both hands, practically between her breasts. "Nothing," I say. "And he probably won't as long as you're here."

"Really? I think he did. I think you get him off. Hey," she says. I don't answer her. "Look at me."

I take a long sip on my beer. She pushes closer so when I lower my hand I brush her nipple with my knuckles.

"Leave me alone," I say.

"Why are you so scared?" I can hear the light bulb over us. "You want to be Toine's girl? You can't be, you know. You can't be someone's girl." I take a step back from her and bump against the cabinet.

"I was born here in Amsterdam," she says. "Two weeks ago, I was barricaded inside of a house and there were men on the other side of the door with torches and guns. Maybe you read about what happened. It turned out they were sponsored by the government. I was sure I was going to die and all I thought about was what I had done to Toine. Have you ever cared about someone that much?"

"No. Not really." I wonder if it's true.

"Look at me, Theo."

"What about what he did to you?" A cockroach scurries behind the fridge. Maybe Toine isn't coming back here at all. Maybe it's time I go back to America.

"Look what he's become. There's nothing left of him. I don't know what else I can do. I'm not going to spend the rest of my life trying to fix him." She dumps the rest of the wine into the sink and it splashes over the sides and across the faucet. She drops the glass into the garbage. "Stop looking like that. You're

like a scared child. I'm not going to try to do anything about it."
I'm wondering what she's referring to, what it is she had planned that she's no longer going to do.

It's almost morning. I feel her weight pressing over the blanket. I wake, then I startle.

"What are you doing?" Jessie is lying next to me, naked, on top of the blanket. I scroll over her body with my eyes as I adjust to the dark. I stare from her ribs to her belly button, over her stomach to the mound of black pubic hair between her legs. Her pressure on the blanket forces the sheet across my shoulders. I'm also naked, but covered. I pull my arm out. The apartment is cold. The windows must be open. She smells unshowered and sweet. There's a key turning in the lock. The moment quickly passes where I can push her away.

"I want him to see me like this." So calm, she stares into the ceiling.

"Don't use me that way. What about me?"

"You're not losing anything. I'm doing you a favor."

"I am losing something. No."

The door opens and then the kitchen light goes on. The yellow light twists its way around the corner and over us. The refrigerator opens then closes. I feel the outline of Jessie's hips through the sheet with my fingertips. Toine's dark silhouette crowds the doorframe. From the floor he seems eight feet tall. Jessie parts her legs just the slightest bit, bends her knees up, reaches forward for her ankles. The room has the dry smell of a hospital. In his shadow all I can make out is the smile spilling across Toine's lips, before he retreats into the other room.

* * *

The show is the same as always. We're in the balcony. Down below, Lucy, with her legs scissored, cigar between them, blows puffs of smoke into the rafters.

"Amsterdam is like nowhere else," I say.

Toine motions toward Rynant with his pinky finger and leans toward me while nodding at the stage. "He has to clean that every night. How do you think he does it?"

Rynant sees Toine pointing at him and bellows, "Homie number one!" Rynant is the strong man in the circus, furrows of skin on his face like a Chinese bulldog. He hoists a keg of beer on either shoulder and marches them down the stairs. I'm drinking whiskey tonight, since we can drink whatever, and Taco clucks at me and shakes his head, smiling. Nothing matters to anyone.

"How could you leave this?" Toine says, waving his arm before him. "Are you sure you can't be converted? Nowhere else in the world."

"Stop it," I say. "It's not fun anymore." Winter is coming soon and when winter comes there will be no more work for anyone except Toine and one or two of the others. Jessie has left. Toine and I watched her from the couch. She folded her clothes carefully into two bags and then stood with one in each hand. Toine was as happy as I had ever seen him. I thought he was going to clap.

"You're like a stone," she said to Toine. She wasn't even looking at me. She left the door open and I considered running after her.

An American woman, older and thick with bleached blond hair, someone who was probably never beautiful, is standing in the audience and has taken off her shirt. She's hefting her breasts in her hands and pushing them to her face where she tries, unsuccessfully, to lick her own nipples. Her lipstick is heavy and her rouge is too thick. She climbs to the stage knees first, where the lesbians have just finished. She strips and sits on the edge and spreads her legs for everyone to see inside of her. This happens sometimes.

If I had the courage of conviction I would ask Toine why he wants me to stay when we are only days away from when he moves out. He knows I would stay if he would stay with me. Since that night he never walks to work with me and we don't have dinner together anymore. I told him I was sorry and he waved away my apology. "Don't apologize for other people," he said. We still see each other in the evenings. His jacket is open now and his shirt unbuttoned at the top. He wants me to stay in that apartment alone so he can come and check on me. Toine likes misery. We all like different things.

Hank returns from the back wearing the gorilla suit, waving around the big plastic penis and the crowd is laughing and clapping. The man the American woman came with, her husband I guess, watches her on the stage. He looks like Peter O'Toole, a thin mustache stuck across his upper lip. Hank gets down in front of the lady and enters her with the gorilla dick.

"Look at that," Toine says. "An American being fucked by a gorilla." The lady puts her hands against his chest and puckers her lips. Music is playing loudly and people are clapping. The woman is clawing at the mask until it comes off and she sees Hank's black face and screams. He looks to the laughing crowd and smiles sheepishly. She struggles out from under him.

"That's what I love about you Americans," Toine says. "You'll fuck a gorilla before a black."

"That lady," I say. I want to say something so profane that it cripples her but I can't find the right words. The day after Jessie left I went to see Adel and gave her half of what I had. She was wearing a white body suit and asked how I knew her name and I said Toine told me. She said everybody knew her name so it didn't matter.

"I'm not going to take my clothes off for you," she said. "You're like a dog." Then she fashioned a collar and a leash around my neck and led me down the stairs. She took me to a room below street level, with linoleum walls, where there was a changing table and a crib. I laid naked on the changing table and she smeared me in Vaseline then dressed me in large diapers. She tied straps around my knees, locked my wrists into the table, and placed two leather pads next to my ears so I couldn't move my head. She stuck a pin through my nipple and I let out a steady moan. She burned me first with candle wax, but then lowered the candle to my body and I caught my breath as the hair on my chest sizzled. She quickly pulled the candle away, lit a cigarette with it. She pulled up on the piercing while pressing the lit cigarette into my chest. She did it over and over again until I couldn't stop screaming. She held my nose closed and dropped the cigarette into my mouth. I left an hour later, my chest covered in burns, my mind clear.

Yuen has turned on all of the lights and Hank's wife is on the stage and Hank is holding her in his furry gorilla arms to stop her from attacking the American woman. As the American is leaving, pulling her husband behind her, I lean over the balcony and launch my glass toward her. The whiskey lands on her head and the glass bounces down the aisle and rolls under a seat. She looks into the balcony, loosing a string of curse words. Toine's hand searches through my collar. "What's gotten into you tonight?" he whispers into my shirt. "This is no way to act."

It's December and a light snow falls. The barkers who stay at work have the bottom of their shoes lined with rubber. The morning shows are cancelled. The hotels advertise lower prices and many restaurants close for the season. Space frees up in the jails and the thieves who have been waiting to serve their sentences disappear from the streets.

Two days before Christmas my plane lands safely in San Francisco. You can tell a lot about a person's childhood by whether or not they like Christmas. I pass through the gates and customs with my one bag. Toine didn't want to say goodbye. He said it was meaningless since we'd inevitably see each other again. A line of yellow and white cabs wait for fares while the blue shuttles stop in the center of the median and claim their passengers. "Last one," the driver says, shutting the door.

I push my pack into the back of the van. "You're going to love San Francisco," a man says to his companion. "Cleanest air in the world." Then suddenly the man turns to me. "Your first time here?" he asks.

"Yeah," I tell him.

"Business or pleasure?"

I want to shake his hand, ask them where they are staying or if they can show me anything. "Pleasure," I reply.

CHAPTER FOUR

MY WIFE

JOE PUNCHED PETEY square in the face and Petey's nose exploded and his blood hit the garbage cans and a garage door. Petey tried to get up but Joe kicked his feet out from under him and his head cracked on the entryway to someone's garage. Then Joe stamped all over his legs and hit Petey over the head with a garbage can lid, then a bottle, which put Petey out for good until the ambulance came. At least that's how I heard it. Someone at the bar said he had it coming. `

"Guess we won't be seeing Petey around anymore," Marco says, raising yet another beer, showing off the burn on his forearm where his tattoo used to be. Someone puts a song on. The pool players continue to shoot. Honey, who always sits on the end near the jukebox in a tight shirt with a leopard print across it, says, "Ain't that a shame?"

I order another beer, one more than I usually have.

"That's my boy," Marco says, slamming his bottle on the counter so the foam pours out, covering his fist. "Let's live a little."

Petey had been stalking Joe's girlfriend, Maria. He's been stalking Maria for years. When Maria and I lived together in that yellow efficiency over Jonquil I'd look out the window at night and see Petey's cigarette burning on the corner. I knew he was staring up at the window and that he saw me looking at him. I knew he was waiting for Maria to walk to the front of the room where our little half-fridge stood. There were trees on that street with gym shoes swaying in the branches, and a park across from the building where the twins hung out, sitting there all night on the monkey bars.

"He bothers me," Maria would say from behind one of her books, sitting on the couch she'd pushed away from the window as far as possible. I'd watch Petey out there and wonder why he wouldn't just go away. And at some point Maria and I would crawl onto the mattress, below the lip of the windowsill. I'd slide my arm around her shoulders and pull her into me, smell her brittle hair, feel the thick scar across her back fitting into my ribcage.

"I have an old friend," I tell Zahava. My wife is sitting at the table in the dining room with a calculator and papers spread out in front of her. She's studying them, pushing them this way and that, like a puzzle. I'm leaning against the doorframe with my head on the wall and she looks up at me and there's color in her cheeks as if she'd just been for a run. "He got beat up really bad tonight."

"I'm sorry, sweetheart," Zahava says. She takes her glasses off and pulls on the bridge of her nose. She has large cheeks and her eyes become small. She's thin, but with wide hips, and she uncrosses her legs as she turns toward me.

"When we were kids, I used to stand on his bed to look out the window. We had a falling out a while ago. He has this weird face that was just dying to get hit. Got beat up all the time. We were roommates for years. When I was locked up. I've told you about that."

"I'm sorry," Zahava says again, placing a hand over the papers, holding the corner of the paper between her thumb and finger, not wanting to let go of it. "I know you had a hard time growing up."

"Me? I didn't have a hard time." I unzip my jacket and throw it over the chair.

"Can you hang that up, please?"

"You can't imagine. Petey got beat up so many times he didn't even care anymore. Petey had a hard time growing up. Compared to him, nobody had a hard time growing up."

Zahava stands and passes me, letting out a patient breath, picking up my jacket and walking it to the closet. She crosses the glass cabinet, which is something her grandmother left her. There are dishes in there that we never use. "Was he nice?" she asks, buried in the closet.

"What's that got to do with anything?"

"I'm just trying to gauge if he brought it on himself or what the circumstances were. And then I intend on getting some work done. Try not to give me a hard time." She crosses back to her seat at the table.

"He was plenty nice," I say. "He never did anything to anyone. So there goes your theory."

"Fine," she says. She returns to her papers, pen in hand. This conversation is finished.

The bathroom is down a hall, before the kitchen. We live in a long two-bedroom apartment on the third floor not too far from the lake and the El. We keep the apartment clean. We used to stay in a smaller place on the ground floor where we were robbed three times, but that was before we were married. *Was he nice?* I run water over my face and sit down on the toilet. I think of my wife smiling and comfortable, drifting along with the crowds downtown. There's a little rack next to the toilet where Zahava puts her magazines when she's through with them. I stare between my legs into the toilet water.

Zahava's eyes are closed and the light is off. I sniff at her armpit. I slide my hand up her leg. Zahava makes a quiet noise, like a giggle. "Sweet baby," she whispers, parting her legs as I press between them with my palm. I lay my palm on top of her vagina and gently slide a finger inside of her. We keep our sex toy in an orange shoebox beneath the bed. We bought it together at Fantasy Makers on Broadway. I pull the box out, take the vibrator from the box. The moon is full tonight and the shades are up. I rub my face along her side and over her breast and kiss her cheek. Zahava places her hand on top of my head. The vibrator looks like a mermaid and a dolphin comes off the side, meant to stimulate the clitoris. The top half of the vibrator is filled with silver balls that rotate around inside a silicone casing for easy washing. Zahava also likes oral sex and sometimes I do that. I consider doing it now. I run the vibrator along the outside of her vagina and I feel her fingers tense in my hair. She knows I like it when she pulls my hair.

Zahava takes her hand from my head and grips the sheets. She slides down and the vibrator sinks and disappears between her legs and then out. Her head presses into her pillow.

Zahava lets out a low moan. I press my hand onto her stomach and spread my fingers over her bellybutton. She came here from Texas to attend law school. At the firm where she works, she puts in long hours but she doesn't complain. I pull the blanket over my head; it's dark and hot. Her legs are spread in shadow in front of me. I kiss my wife's nipple and I watch the toy come in and out of her black pubic hair. We'll both have to go to work in the morning.

I board the train at Morse and head toward the loop. Sometimes I switch at Belmont to the purple line, which drops me closer to my office. Other times I don't bother. I ride the old north-south through the city that I've always lived in, through Edgewater, Lakeview, Lincoln Park. I watch the streets get cleaner until Fullerton, where the train ducks underground. If I were to stay on the train, like I did when I was fifteen, then when the train rose back above ground I would see a switch. As the train reached Cermak the last white people would get off. At Thirty-fifth I'd be at the hard corners of Stateway Gardens. After that the streets are wider and the buildings are like broken teeth. At Fifty-fifth I would have gotten off the train and attempted to walk to my home, through the Vice Lords and the El Rukns. And sometimes I would make it and sometimes I wouldn't.

I stop in the cafeteria at the bottom of the building and buy a coffee and a bagel, and head upstairs. Jim Thompson, the for-mer governor of Illinois, has an office in this building and one time I saw him in the elevator. He was six-and-a-half feet tall and wearing an olive green suit. He had a smooth fat face and thin red hair and looked like an angry child. I said hello.

I put my bagel and coffee on the desk, turn on my comput-er, check for internal company memos. There have been layoffs recently. I wait for my name to come up. I figure they don't pay me enough to fire me. I'm a senior file clerk and sometimes I joke with Zahava that I'm in charge of the alphabet. "Don't misplace any letters," she'll say, laughing. "We need all of them." But it's more than just alphabetizing. Employees are ranked by skill set and necessity, factors that determine the color of their folders. The senior executives occupy entire cabinets along the top while admins and messengers are crammed into small drawers close to the floor. It would seem like a joke except that a couple of years ago when I tried to change the layout of the cabinets, placing a handful of janitors in the third tier and a vice president closer to the floor, I was reprimanded by my supervisor. There are thousands of green cabinets with thousands of records in each, documenting every employee that has ever worked here since the company was founded in 1933, during the Depression.

I finger through the papers. Feel a tap on my shoulder. "Happy Friday, Theo."

Jim is my temp. He's twenty-two years old. He just graduated from DePaul and we're contracting him from Sally Girl. He may or may not stick around. "Jim," I say. "I think today we should organize F."

For years I've been seeing a professional dominatrix. Her dungeon studio is on the second floor of an industrial building, near the Lake Street train. Next door is an Irish bar where first-time customers are expected to call in from the downstairs payphone. I remember the first day I came to see her, during the Gulf War. She wrapped me in Saran Wrap so I couldn't even move my fingers. She slapped me lightly, then pulled a mask over my head. The mask had a long tube coming off of it so I couldn't see, and she whispered that there was nothing I could do. Then she pinched the tube and I couldn't breathe. It felt like I was relaxing for the first time in my life. I usually go on Fridays but recently it hasn't been working for me. Recently it hasn't even been close.

I sit naked in an airy waiting room with my hands folded into my lap, my clothes in front of me in a wicker hamper.

There's a large desk with a rotary-dial phone on it, a bowl full of mints. On the wall a single black and white photo of a dark-skinned woman, a whip curled around her body like a snake. A blond lady comes in carrying a riding crop. She's new. She's tall, six feet at least, with enormous breasts and wide hips. "Let's go," she says, snapping her finger in front of my nose.

I follow her, carrying the wicker hamper through two rooms full of medical equipment, rubber masks with plastic eyes and long snouts, masks shaped like dog's heads, enema bags, baby cribs, cages, and into a third room which is populated with a padded wooden table, two large thrones with throw rugs in front of them, a leather hammock with metal chains at the end of it, walls full of whips and strap-on dildos. "On the table," the blond lady says. "Now." I climb onto the table, face down. She yanks straps around my ankles. "Lower," she says. "Wider." She pulls on my legs, then my wrists. She pulls me around like a doll. Then her hand comes down heavily on my back. "Maybe I'll have to come back and watch you," she says. "Are you an exhibition-ist?" I nod my head while sucking in on my lips. "I might like that." And then she leaves.

The table is cold, especially against my genitals. I wait for the familiar clap of Mistress Jade's heels tapping the floor. She usually leaves me like this for ten minutes before coming in. The hospital is a long way. I'll go there from here. Today was a bad day at work. Everything is bad recently. They used to get Petey in the bathroom with towels full of soap bars, over his head and in his stomach, drumming him with their heavy bags. He'd end up lying on the tile floor, his face full of blood, trying to smile, the blood running in rivulets through his teeth. I'd wash myself in the corner slot and stare at him lying there. He was this deformed white animal.

I hear the knocking and the long slide of a metal latch, the door opening as Mistress Jade walks in. Then I see her, standing in front of me, latex shorts, thick brown legs. I stare straight ahead, to the top of her thighs, her voice above me. "What have we got here? Look at him. Oh, he looks so funny." I hear the other girl, the blond one, laughing. Mistress Jade walks away from my field of vision. "What is this?" Mistress Jade's hand searches between my legs, grabbing, holding, and then squeezing, my body arching up to give her a better grip, the familiar, painful squeeze shooting into my stomach. "Look, he's getting hard. He's a pervert. You want to use this? I don't think so. Hmm, hmm, hmm."

The other girl's hands are pressing firmly on the sides of my face, her fingers pinching my ears. She's wearing a strap-on dildo. She rubs it under my nose. Mistress Jade is wrapping a cord around my penis. I open my lips and the dark silicone head of the dildo pushes toward the back of my throat, making me gag. Mistress Jade pulls the cords tight and I let out a muffled scream. "Come on now, sissy. Sissy, sissy boy."

Petey is alone in a pasta-colored hospital room just south of Bryn Mawr Avenue, the bed next to him empty. In the homes, we were never alone, squeezed into rooms on mattress quotas. When we got out we all swam away. He's watching the little TV up on the stand above him and shuts it off when I come in. He has dark yellow circles under his eyes, bandages across the middle of his face. Both legs in casts. When he smiles I see the missing teeth, but he was missing teeth already.

"Theo," he says, with that absurd, uncomprehending voice he has. *We'll do everything together.* "You came to see me."

I shake my head, put the flowers on the stand next to him, and sit on the window ledge with my hands folded in my lap.

The view below is flat roofs and smokestacks. A nurse walks by the room pulling a four-wheeled dolly full of plates and urine samples.

"Why wouldn't I?"

"Doctor says I'll be out in a couple of weeks. Check this out. I press this button and it injects morphine. Want to try? I'll dose you up. It's *craaaazy,* man."

"They gave you morphine." I smile and I consider it, but I don't do it. We met in Western when I was twelve and Petey fifteen. I shouldn't have been there. The walls were soundproofed and the doors locked from the outside. Petey had been stealing cars and driving them around Park Ridge and Elmhurst. He took them from the city and drove them out to the suburbs where there are houses with green lawns and trees in front. He watched the mothers send their children off to private schools.

When they brought him to my room I raised my hands and folded my arms over my head. "Don't come near me," I told him. He was the ugliest kid I had ever seen. I had my own problems. "I haven't shot dope in years," I say, plucking the needle from his arm, wiping the blood on my pants. I make a fist and squeeze my forearm. With my other hand I push the pin into my wrist and Petey presses the button. It feels nice, like a hand over your face.

"That's all you can get for ten minutes. Better take the needle out." I pull the needle out and smile at Petey. The IV hangs between us. He presses the button and morphine squirts on the floor. "I guess you could have gotten more," Petey says. "Hee hee."

I shake my head. "Big Petey." The words come out of my mouth slowly, my lips are stuck. "You never win any fights," I say, rubbing my chin and my cheeks, trying to stretch my face. "I bet you spend more time getting beat up than you do sleeping. You always got beat up."

"Not like you," he says. "You had protection."

"What's that supposed to mean?" I say, still shaking my head, leaning into the window, comforted by the glass and the rising smoke from below. We've never talked about Mr. Gracie before. Mr. Gracie, bringing me back into the room every Tuesday night. Afterward, the long walk back through the corridors of the ward. The electric buzz of the hallways. The rooms locked from the outside and the boys sleeping. Mr. Gracie walking behind me but still hovering on my back, then unlocking my door and closing the door behind me. The rumble of the lock. Petey lying awake, waiting for me. His eyes like mirrors. The high wears off quick as it came. I clear my throat and try to be the voice of reason. "My wife, you know."

"You didn't invite me to your wedding," he says, like it's our own private joke.

"I didn't invite anybody to my wedding. It wasn't much, just her family, some friends of hers from school. Wet chicken." Petey leans forward, as if he was going to sit up on his elbows, then winces and slowly leans back into the pillows.

"Tell me about your wife."

"We were married in Houston. Mosquitoes the size of elbows and smog like soup. You can't even see the sky. It's the worst place I've ever been. I never thought a city could be that ugly."

"Was it bugly?" he asks. "Butt ugly?"

"It was fugly," I tell him. "Fucking ugly. Don't be an idiot. Stop following Maria. That guy she's with, he's an animal. It's not safe."

"What's your wife's name?"

I put my hand up. "No one expects the Spanish Inquisition," I say. Petey smiles, then winces again. It occurs to me that it's my fault. "Zahava," I say. "You'd like her. Everybody does. She's easy to like. She smiles a lot. She likes to have a good time. She used to do a lot of cocaine but she doesn't anymore. That was a long time ago." I shake my head. "Really, Petey, leave Maria alone."

Petey makes a movement that resembles a shrug of the shoulders. "I love her," he says, as if it were the most simple thing in the world and the smell of the hospital had nothing to do with it, as if anybody who walks away from love is a fool, and I know as soon as he gets out of here he'll be standing outside her window again, hoping for a breeze carrying some of Maria's scent. Maria smells like cheap lotion from a Jergens bottle, peaches, which is what her skin feels like where there aren't scars. And Joe will kill Petey, because that's the kind of guy Joe is.

I came home one day to an empty efficiency and I knew Maria was gone for good. She'd been going out more and more, leaving the apartment in a short skirt with no underwear, the wind biting at her blue-veined legs. Heading down to the gas station, getting in cars. She'd come home with bruises, black eyes, a bloody nose.

"Don't go out, Maria."

"What do you know? Stop me." What she was really saying was, Make it stop.

I made my own trips, to the Wasteland, but everything's different. I was nineteen years old and knew less than I do now. I'd squeeze into Maria's clothes when she was gone, take the stairs in stockings, walk the streets in her underwear, mascara around my eyes. The girls in front of the bookstore ignored me. The gangsters near Howard just laughed. "Hey bitch, you want to suck my dick?" I'd run from them. Sometimes I'd stop. Sometimes they'd catch me. I didn't know what I wanted and Maria wouldn't stay home. I cried when she showed up with hash marks cut across her chest. They were over her breasts and belly, thin diagonal slices. Red, with bits of blood on the edges. Her body looked like it had been hog-tied in razor wire.

"Who did this?"

"I wanted it."

We'd look at each other sometimes, both of us beat up, neither of us able to protect the other one. We'd stare at each other with as much space as the small mattress would allow. Two years ago she called me at work. She was back in the neighborhood. She wanted me to meet her new boyfriend. She wanted to know what I thought.

We sat in the back room of a bar on a cobbled street by Loyola University, the kind of place where old men order beer by the pitcher. Maria looked fit and healthy for the first time in her life. She wore skintight leggings and a shirt that stopped at her waist. She kept her eyes low. The guy she was with had muscles coming out of his neck and shoulders like a car grille. She went to hug me and he grabbed her by the hair. She lightly patted my shoulder with one hand instead. I decided to ignore it. We had two beers and spoke in generalities about things like the cement border the alderman erected in the middle of Howard Street. When I asked Maria where she had been she said, "Around." Joe yanked her chair over to his and she looked at her hands. He spoke for her.

"She was in Wisconsin, working in the Oshkosh factory in Apple. OK. We live behind the Heartland." He glared at me. He said he worked out six days a week and flexed his arms to show me that he meant it. He said he knew how to kick-box. "Theo, or whatever your name is," he said. "Maria had a hard childhood. Everybody has a hard childhood. I had a hard childhood. I used to get beat up a lot, believe it or not." He talked like he had been sucking gas with pebbles in his mouth. "You know what I did to the people that used to beat me up when I was a kid? I found them later and I put them in the hospital. Every last one of them."

I sipped my beer and stared up at the bar TV. I wondered why Maria wanted me to meet him. Did she want me to save her? Or did he put her up to it? On the TV the Bulls were playing the Pistons. It was the playoffs.

The next day Maria called. I had to take the call at my boss's desk. I didn't have my own desk. "He hits me. You wouldn't do that."

"I hit you sometimes."

"Not the way I like it."

"I didn't want to leave bruises."

"I like bruises. I don't want to make any more decisions."

I pulled at the pens near the filing cabinets. I took a pen and pulled the cap off, then put the cap back on. Where I was sitting I could see a sliver of lake from the window not too far away. My boss kept a metal pencil sharpener on her desk shaped like the Eiffel Tower. "I don't like it," I said. "He's a monster. I bet he can't even add."

"You're jealous," she said, and I could hear that same anger in her voice. "You want the same thing so don't judge me. You wish someone would tell you what to do. If you could find a girl to make your decisions you would let her. We're the same." She was waiting for me to deny it. To tell her what she had with Joe was garbage. That she was just another abused housewife.

"I still don't like it," I told her. "It's a stupid way to think."

"It's not thinking at all," she said. "That's the point." That was the last time we spoke and Maria was the only girl I ever loved.

*   *   *

75

"That's two nights staying out late," Zahava says. "You're a wild man these days." She's putting dishes up in the cabinet. The papers that were all out on the table last night have been put away and replaced by a thin leather bag. As she reaches up, her shirt rises and I see her thin pale stomach, the small muscles on her back squeezed together by the belt of her jeans. She's getting better looking as she's getting older. She wasn't very pretty when we first met in a restaurant near the university four years ago. I was cashiering and she was waiting tables. She had another boyfriend then. I was working two jobs, night and day. Zahava was about to start law school. We sat at the bar at night, having drinks. Then we'd go out, the whole restaurant, all the waiters and the bartender and dishwashers. We'd go to clubs down on Belmont where we'd dance or sit at the bar with our chin in our fists. There were a lot of habits in that restaurant. One person died, others left town or went to rehab. Others got straight and got married. We don't go out together anymore. We see each other at home. I take off my backpack and lay it by the door.

"I stopped to see Petey in the hospital. He looks terrible." I pass to where we keep a Jack Daniels bottle on the second shelf. I have the urge to wrap my arms about her waist and kiss the back of her neck but I grab the bottle instead, pour a splash into a glass and top it with an ice cube. I move into the living room. Turn the TV on. There's an ad for *Home Alone 2*. There was no concern in Zahava's voice. I could have stayed out for a month and it wouldn't have mattered. She's been cheating on me for a while now. A guy she works with, Mickey. An athletic-looking guy, tall, with thick black hair, strong features, high cheekbones. I get up, change the channel. This couch has gotten soft and old. How did this happen? She thinks I don't know but she leaves her checkbooks open. They do it at a pay-by-the-hour hotel just west of downtown.

Not counting Petey, Marco is my last friend from the homes. Though we're not really friends. He once led a group of kids who pissed on my clothes when I was out of the room. We drink together sometimes. We have several beers and we talk about Petey. One time, during a riot, Petey, Marco, and I stood back to back to create a "triangle." It worked. When it was all over and the place was locked down, we were unscathed. Now Marco is heavyset. He works in the fish department at a high-end grocery in Lincoln Park.

"Joe holds the door at Pine Lodge," Marco says. "If you're curious."

"That's right on the border," I say. "No man's land."

"Only four a.m. for miles," Marco says. "And to the north of there it's dry."

I grab a napkin and scribble out a map. Eight lines, cross-hatches, a taxi stand, then nothing. There are two pool tables now in the back of Carrie's. Several groups of men hang back there, some with their own sticks, flames shooting up the wood. I shake my head, so bewildered by the things people do.

"Why don't you go see Petey?" I say. "He hasn't had any visitors."

Marco waves his hand. "Payday mayday," he says when the bartender comes over. "Did you visit me when I was in prison? How about a shot." The bartender lays one shot of dark orange liquid in front of Marco and he raises his eyebrow and I nod and he puts a shot in front of me. Marco flicks his fingers and the shot disappears. He shakes his head. "Oogly oogly oogly, aaah," he says. "Of course he hasn't had any fucking visitors. He's a loser."

"There's an obligation."

"The statute of limitations has long since run out on any obligations I might have."

* * *

On the very edge of Chicago, before a taxi stand, and then a gulch, and then the flickering lights of St. Francis followed by the wealthy North Shore, there's a twenty-four-hour Walgreens. Next to the Walgreens is a Jewel grocery store with a big, juicy orange sign. Next to that a shoe repair, a Ben Franklin General Store, and at the end of all of that a Bakers Square, and then the Pine Lodge.

Late at night there are maybe twenty cars in the parking lot, all of them driving home drunk come four in the morning. I walk through the parking lot and feel the weight of the city pressing into my shoulders. Joe sits on a stool, his large frame dwarfing the chair legs, in jeans and a leather shirt, waiting as people come up to the bar, identification in hand. I wonder where all of these people come from, like ants crawling from a Howard Street sand hill, to go to this bar so late at night. I think of the news footage last night of the houses on the Malibu cliffs and the waves bucking against the hills and the mudslides and the houses falling into the ocean.

I hand Joe my ID and he looks at it and he recognizes me. "Didn't think I'd see you again," he says. His voice is higher than when we first met, and the muscles in his forehead seem to be forcing themselves over his eyes. "You sure do wait awhile. Maria said you're a coward and you would never have the guts to come around."

"Maria knows me best," I say, shoving my hands into my pockets. He drops my card onto the ground and looks the other way. I bend down to pick it up, smelling the leather of his black boots, my nose practically running over the laces. He shifts his foot slightly on the lower rail, the chair-rung squeals, and I close my eyes.

I wade into the bar, which holds only a little more light than the outside. Buzzing neon signs hang on the windows and the walls, accompanying the incessant ringing of the poker machines, of which there are three. I look above the bobbing heads, trying to spot Maria.

"Are you or aren't you," the bartender asks. She's beefy and blond and I take her right away for the owner of the place.

"I am," I tell her. "I'll have a Budweiser." I push her my five dollars and she places a bottle in front of me. So now I have a weapon. I leave seventy-five cents on the bar and walk back near the bathrooms and the pool table, where Maria is sitting mostly alone, not far from the dartboard. And it seems to me for a minute like she wants to get hit by the dart and that's why she's sitting there. But she isn't available, and people obviously know that. And she sits in front of a glass of clear liquid. And there's a tiny lamp on the bar. And she's reading by it.

"Anything interesting?" I ask. She turns the book down and looks up at me, her face a mixture of embarrassment and surprise. It's one in the morning. Years have passed.

"You're making a mistake coming here."

"Of course I am." I pull my hand from the bar and wipe the residue on my pants. "Time waits for no man," I say, trying to make a joke. "My father used to say that." I drink my beer down quickly. For courage. I take in her dark cheeks. Maria has round features, round sad eyes, a round face. She used to tell me she looked like a housecleaner, which simply isn't true. I think she looks like a schoolteacher.

"I'm just shocked," she says. "Wow." My throat feels tight and I wonder how I'm going to breathe. "Wow," shaking her head. After a bit Maria says, "I'm working at the library again."

"I'm still working at the same place," I say. "But I took a break to work in a restaurant once." I feel my body bending toward her.

"That advertising company or whatever?"

"Yeah."

We don't say anything for a little while, and then a few guys behind us knock a pitcher of beer off a table and Joe comes storming back. "What the fuck's going on?" But he's talking to the guys that spilled the beer. One of the beer signs makes a quick, piercing sound and shuts off.

"What's it like?" I ask.

"What's it like? It's wonderful," she responds. "I still see Nadia. I'm not allowed to have guy friends. You know, he gets jealous easy, which I like. I have to tell him everything I do and everywhere I go." I nod. Wait for her to continue. "He tucks me in at night, makes sure I brush my teeth in the morning. He does these things for me. It's hard to explain. We have an entire setup in the basement. And he's nice to me, though I suppose he'll beat me around quite a bit tonight. But he really is nice. It's better than the alternative. I was going to kill myself." She puts her hand on the bar and turns it over so I can see her wrist. We both stare at her wrist together. It's like a one-way map.

"It's kind of a funny compulsion, huh?" And I feel that warmth of nostalgia. The red neon is backlighting her hair, the tiny yellow light surrounding her cheeks.

I lift my hand, intent on pushing her hair back. "Don't," she says.

"You don't have to be with that guy," I say. "There's other things."

Maria laughs a little bit and raises her hand as if she was going to touch my cheek. "You're a hero now?"

"I went to visit Petey. He's not going to walk again."

Maria looks down into her drink. I signal for another one and I'm sure the bartender sees but she ignores me. "There was a restraining order out," Maria says quietly. "He wasn't supposed to be anywhere near me. The police ruled it self-defense."

"That was hardly self-defense."

"We haven't seen each other in years and this is what you want to talk about."

"Maybe I want to talk about you leaving after you said you never would," I say.

Maria looks at me like I'm a stray dog with rabies. "Don't do this."

"Don't you remember? We all promised."

"We were a group of kids when we said that. And we didn't mean it. That was before Petey was following me to the grocery store. And you gave away all of our money. And before Tom overdosed and died and Larry went to jail. And Cateyes died because nobody bothered to check. No wonder his eyesight kept getting worse—it was cancer. All those promises are shit. The group homes," she says. She says *group homes* quietly and with such contempt that it rings right through my bones. "Who could blame anybody for wanting to forget?"

When I feel Joe's fingers pinching my neck I swing my bottle at him, which is about the bravest thing I've ever done, but I miss. He catches the bottle in his hand and casually dumps it into the trash. He pulls me through the bar and the patrons make way for us and the bartender wipes out her glasses and doesn't even pretend to look up. Joe pushes me into the parking lot, under the phosphorescence. I stumble, nearly fall, catch myself with my hands on the asphalt. I turn, raising my arm, and expect to get hit but he's standing ten feet behind me at his post at the door.

"Get out of here," he says.

The parking lot is empty. "You can't do what you did," I say.

"Leave us alone, jackass. We're happy. Don't try to interrupt us." He's not afraid of me at all. I brush my pants and feel where the gravel has cut my hands. Joe is buttoning his shirt. He doesn't think I'm going to do anything, and I realize that he's right. The night out here, on the edge of nowhere, nothing but the sounds of a taxi making the rounds. Everybody is either in the bar or home asleep. In the whole world it's just me and Joe.

My wife sleeps quietly in the bed. The room is full of her breathing. Then she moves, exposing her pale ankles. She's questioned her decisions before. Sometimes she says that maybe being a lawyer wasn't the best idea for her. I pull the belt from my pants and place it on the dresser. Take my shirt off, my pants. Stand naked, watching my wife. I pick my belt off the dresser. I watch her movements. Watch her wake up. Her small eyes opening slowly. The way she looks at me. Naked, with a belt in my hand, in front of her.

"I want you to tie this belt around my neck," I say, the belt hanging limply over my hand. "And drag me around with it like a leash. I want you to choke me. I want you to spit on me. I want you to slap me and call me names."

A wave of panic crosses Zahava's face and then leaves. "What are you talking about? Turn on the light."

"Please," I say.

Zahava considers my words. "I have to be in court tomorrow. Come here." She slides down to the end of the bed. I hand her the belt and stand in front of her, turning around, pressing my fingers into the wall. I hold my breath and then the belt whips across my back. I feel the sting and my mind goes blank for a second, the warmth of pain covering me as my breath returns.

"It's OK," she says, rubbing her hand over where she's just hit me, tracing the welt with her finger. Then the belt lands again, then again. My back burns. She hits me five times and then she stops. She pinches a bit of my lower back and twists.

"Ow. Ow."

"Now let's go to sleep, sweetness." She's touching me, her hands at my waist.

I sit down on the floor and Zahava sighs. She slips from her blanket and her feet are on either side of me and I place my head in her lap, my arms around her waist.

"What's happening to you, Theo? You know?" She's awake now, as calm as a lawyer. "You're not acting like yourself. I know you like these things. So what? People need different things." She pauses. Zahava has a sour smell. "People need their attorneys to be on time and to be rested as well. Don't be selfish. Please." I press my face into her pubic hair. She keeps saying things like, "What happened tonight? Did something happen?" But it's like she's talking through water and I can't hear a word she's saying. And I'm thinking about where the highways will take me.

"Why do you cheat on me?" I ask.

"Hey," she says. "Hey." Now she is really pulling my hair, trying to get me out of her, jerking my head back and forth. "We've been through this before." She's looking me square in the eyes. "Just stop it." I keep my mouth shut.

"Please," I say quietly, rolling my bottom lip over.

She lets go of me and I drift back between her legs. The smell of Zahava's legs, her thighs against my cheeks. How she smells inside. She's so thin I can feel the bones in her legs. I feel the pressure of her fingers against my scalp. "Enough, Theo." She's trying to pull me up and I'm resisting, pushing my face further against her vagina. "You're selfish. You know? You never think of anyone else."

CHAPTER FIVE

GETTING IN GETTING OUT

THERE'S A LARGE woman in front of me in a white dress with dark flowers. She smells like baby powder and she's holding the hand of a small girl whose red hair is scattered across her shoulders to make her look like a doll. The two of them are not related. It's early in the morning and it's a thick, slow line and nobody in it is in a hurry. The girl tries to say something and the lady reaches down and brushes her lips with her index finger.

At the edge of the table I empty my pockets into a Tupperware dish, step through the metal detector with my hands out and my palms open. The police officer nods, slides my belongings across a barren steel table, a set of keys and a wallet with a chain that attaches to my belt loop. I'm too young to be a parent, too old to be in trouble. I pour my things from the dish into my hand.

I walk past the courtrooms where the children are tried for crimes committed across the city. Things like robbing parking meters or throwing other children from rooftops. The yellow benches outside the courtrooms are filled today with juveniles waiting for their verdicts. The kids are not allowed in the actual courtroom unless the judge summons them with a question. The violent offenders and the run risks are cuffed to a chair in one-person rooms known as hotboxes.

In the basement there's a cafeteria with eight grey tables, wire chairs, and a vending machine that sells hot chocolate, coffee, and chicken soup from the same spout. I buy a coffee and sit down where someone has left a newspaper. I read about the heat wave and what the newly elected mayor of Chicago plans to do about it. It's the hottest summer on record and people are dying everywhere. Across from me three officers are taking a break. They sit in front of three empty cups. They think I'm on their side. I place my hand over the mayor's face. I run through the plan in my head.

In the years since I've been here they've placed art along the walls of the lower floors. Cityscapes and still-lifes, all of them dirty-looking in cheap metal frames. There's an escalator, and then wider, black, polished stairs leading to the second floor. The top three floors of Western house the jail, a brutal place, always over-crowded and understaffed. Children are supposed to be shipped from here to St. Charles within three months. It doesn't always work that way. Paperwork gets lost. If the parent doesn't show up to collect the child there are proceedings for the child to be made a ward of the court. The state takes custody. A placement has to be found. The placements are run by private agencies like the Jewish Children's Bureau or the Catholic Charities or the Children's Home and Aid Society, who may or may not want the kid the state is offering. The state allocates the same funds, $31 per day per child, whether the child is in a group home, a shelter, or a mental hospital. There are children who spend years in here.

I come to a large door and adjust my tie against my reflection. Inside there's another door, and then another, and the intake for the jail and the administrative offices, where the secretary sits in front to greet and vet visitors. The secretary, years ago, was a beautiful Hispanic woman named Camilla who took everyone's name into a green binder as they were admitted. I never spoke to Camilla but I remember her. Everybody does. She was removed for having an affair with one of the inmates— someone's dream come true. He was seventeen years old, being tried as an adult. It was his last good time. I was twelve then and knew only what I heard in the lunch hall. They were caught in a broom closet with her skirt up around her waist. But there are other places to have sex in Western, unused offices, of course the showers. The doors to the rooms don't have windows and are locked from the outside and it's two to four boys for every room, so opportunity exists there as well.

Camilla is a nice memory for me, though I didn't know her at all. I just remember her red skirt, and the short pointy heels on her shoes, and where her skirt stopped and her legs began. I thought about her every day I was inside and by the time I got out she was gone.

"I'm here to see George Washington." I almost want to laugh. I'm asking about a young black house-robber named for the founder of our country. *It's no wonder you like to steal,* I'll tell him, *you're on every quarter.*

"What's your relation?" the lady asks. She's not pretty, like Camilla, this one. She has wiry black and white hair, piled on her head like a dead nest. She looks dead. She's old and salty. A safe bet, I suppose, a dead woman.

"Caseworker," I tell her. She looks at me skeptically. I'm dressed in black pants and a button-down shirt, my clothes stuck to my skin from the heat outside. "DCFS," I say, to show I know the lingo, speak the language. State not charity. DCFS as opposed to Board of Ed, or HHS or federal, which would be ridiculous but you never know. As opposed to guardian *ad litem*, for which I would have to be a lawyer. And I'm obviously not family. DCFS is easy enough. Department of Children and Family Services and the family-first policy. Caseworkers change all the time. I went through twelve caseworkers before I was eighteen and didn't know who was looking after me. Most of them I never met. I'd just see their name on a piece of paper or they'd call to cancel an appointment.

"They're in the yard now," she says. She must have taken this job to pass the time after retiring, because she was bored. She wanted to spend her final years in a penal institution helping to punish bad children. I wait in front of her, behind the long brown partition. I don't want her to think I'm going to leave and I don't want her to think I have all day. I've thought all my actions through. And I've thought that I could fail. I've imagined them finding me out, coming to me from the sides and behind with a net, pulling a mask over my head, zipping it from the back, taping my hands to my skull, cinching the net around me, and dragging me along the linoleum floors back into a locked white room with a view of the freeway, and leaving me there. Forgetting me again, this time forever. So I wait, tapping my finger lightly on the countertop.

She buzzes the glass door next to her and I grip onto the handle and click inside. The air is like a television tuned to static. I follow her past cubicles, each divided with six-foot-high walls of fabric. Some of the cubicles are empty and others contain people sitting at computers entering data or talking into the phone. This is the administrative heart of the detention center but it isn't necessary. All you need in a jail is inmates and guards. You barely need guards.

* * *

I'm left in a fluorescent room with a table and two chairs, a large ashtray, and a stand with magazines piled across the top of it. I place my notebook on the table and a pencil next to it. Caseworkers always do this. There's always a notebook. I place my hands behind my head and try to relax.

The first time my girlfriend was robbed was three months ago. We had only just started dating. I met her at the restaurant where we work. I have a hard time sleeping and she doesn't like to sleep until morning. She's in law school at Loyola and she waits tables. I had picked up a second job cashiering at the restaurant to keep me busy at night and because of some trouble I was having. That's where I met Zahava.

When she was robbed that time, we were in her bed with the covers off and we heard a sound from outside and she wondered what it was and I said I was sure it was just the cat. When we came out of the room, a few hours later, we were still naked and the bicycle was missing and Zahava's Guatemalan backpack was in the middle of the floor, the front pocket open, her tip money gone. She shook her head and pulled a Lenny Kravitz album from its sleeve. and lowered the needle onto the vinyl. She would have to get another bicycle. She zipped her bag and placed it on the couch. She turned to me and smiled. Easy come, easy go.

I pick up one of the *Men's Journal*s. There's a picture of a man on the cover wearing sky blue shorts and no shirt and he appears to be running up a mountain. He looks healthy and content. His skin is smooth, his chin and cheeks perfect.

I read through the magazine while I'm waiting. It could be a while. There's a whole system of doors and elevators to be negotiated in bringing a child down to the second floor. I read what foods I should eat if I'm going to have a pretty stomach. I learn how to improve my biceps by doing exercises with weights and tucking my elbows tightly beneath my ribs. And I learn that it drives women crazy if you pull on their clitoris gently with your thumb and your forefinger and then blow on it.

When I'm done with the magazine George Washington is in front of me with a guard. The guard doesn't introduce himself. The guard says he's going to lock the door and that I have to ring a bell next to the table to be let out. When I ring the bell someone will come and take George Washington back to the third floor, but it might take a few minutes.

"You're not my caseworker," George Washington says to me as the guard is leaving.

"I am now. Sit down," I tell George. "Let's get to know each other."

He's a small kid. Scrappy. He has a muscular face but skin like a baby. They've given him the haircut, his scalp covered in short, black fuzz. The door clicks and latches and George is looking at me, considering his options. Maybe there is something he could use as a weapon: a piece of metal to be quickly sharpened, a dull, heavy object. He could take me hostage, tell the police that he'll kill me if they don't let him out. They wouldn't deal with him, and when the standoff was over we would both be headed back to jail.

"Cigarette?" I ask, taking the pack from my pocket. He takes the cigarette from me and tucks it behind his ear. He sits down across from me on the other side of the table. I light my cigarette and toss the lighter to him. "You might as well smoke it. They're not going to let you take it back to the floor." He must know this already. How could he not know that? Of course he knows. He's been here weeks already. He considers the lighter but doesn't take it. He leaves the cigarette behind his ear. Was I like this? No. I was scared and obedient. I would have smoked that cigarette down, hands folded into my lap, staring at the floor. And I would have said thank you. That's the kind of child I was. People did whatever they wanted with me. George is strong and defiant. Fuck you, he's saying, the way he crosses his arms across his small chest and stares at the locked door as if it was a personal insult, but he is stronger than the door and through his will he's going to tear the door right from the hinges. There's only one problem with his theory.

"I have a whole pack," I say and push them across the table to him. He picks the pack up, stuffs the lighter inside, and shoves the pack inside the waistband of his pants. Now he's smiling, kind of like the child he is, curious to see what I'll do. I'm not going to do anything. I'll buy a pack at the convenience store where the shuttle stops. They'll search him before taking him back. They'll take his cigarettes from him and divide them amongst themselves. What the fuck, they'll think. What kind of a caseworker would give a juvenile offender a pack of cigarettes?

"So how are they treating you?" I ask. This is the refrain. I learned this over seven years. Every time I met a new caseworker they would ask me how I was being treated and I'd say "Fine," instead of saying "I'm being raped." I'd say "Good" instead of telling them the other boys jumped me and forced a bar of soap into my mouth. I'd say "OK," instead of saying "I hate it here, they won't let me go outside." And they always ask the same question. They don't change a single word. The administrators, guardians, caseworkers, volunteers, hospital staff. Always, "So how are they treating you?" Which is what I ask now, on the other side, but not really. I have a good idea how he is being treated. He's not giving any back mouth to the guards and the guards are ignoring him. In the yard he stands near the pole. He's getting in fights sometimes to prove himself to his gang. At school he's in one of the classes for the kids that can't sit still. I can see it all.

"Listen, you know, I put a lot of effort into getting here today. How old are you?"

"How old are you?" he blurts back. He's gotten tired of the quiet game.

"I'm twenty-three."

"I'm thirteen," he says. Of course he is. It's just the age.

"When's your court date set for?"

"Don't you know?" he asks. He's suspicious. Children in this place are always suspicious.

"I didn't bring my papers with me, so I don't know." He shrugs his shoulders. OK. Fine. I lean back, he leans back. The light hanging over us is dim and fat. I've never been good with kids, not even when I was one. "Give me a cigarette," I say. He looks like he doesn't know what I'm talking about. I don't even know why I'm here. I remember very distinctly standing on Petey's bed two floors up, sometimes stepping on his legs, and looking out the window in our room through a patchwork of wire and saying to myself that if they ever let me out of this place I would never come back. But here I am. For what? To walk the red lines painted on the floor outside the classrooms. For this child who's already stolen my cigarettes, who looks like all of the kids that used to spit on me and beat me up, a smaller version of Larry, the most fearsome kid in Western when I was here. The kid who eventually broke my leg, just days before they let me out. That's what he looks like, this little bastard. He looks like Larry. I shake my head. Consider threatening him. It wouldn't work. It's what he wants. I went through all of this for George Washington. I bought these clothes, dark pants, button-up shirt. Cut my hair, bought this notebook. Took a day off of work, just so I could come here and give this thirteen-year-old asshole some information and now he won't even give me one of my own cigarettes.

"If you don't give me a cigarette," I say, finally, staring into the fixture and the black marks on the ceiling above it, "I'm going to leave, and you're never ever going to find out why I came here or what I meant to tell you."

I can see him thinking about it. Curiosity is a weapon with children. Fear and longing for the unknown. What a horrible little room this is. Smells just like this place, too. Rooms smell different when you can't get out. George relents. He takes the cigarette from behind his ear and rolls it across the table to me. I raise my eyebrow. He pulls the packet out from inside his pants, removing the lighter and placing it on the table then flicking it to me with his index finger. It slides across the table and lands in my palm and I light my cigarette with it and I slide the lighter back to him and he tucks it back in the pack and the pack back inside the waistband of his pants.

"What you want to talk about?" he asks now, lightly drumming on his thighs. "Why you messin' with me?"

"The police," I tell him. "I want to talk to you about the police."

Zahava was robbed a second time, just a couple of weeks later. But we weren't there then. After work we had gone with some of the other restaurant employees over to Sunny's house. There were drugs, as usual. Heroin and cocaine in little white paper packets. Everyone pitched in. Zahava went up and I went down and I was sitting against the wall and everything was in slow motion. Heroin is the only thing that makes me relax. Zahava likes cocaine. She likes to have a good time. It's hurting her grades, she says. But she always wants to go out. She was chatting rapidly with Scales, the bartender. Once, when we were at a bar near Belmont, I saw Zahava tuck her hand into Scales's back pocket. She has better posture than the rest of us, and I thought to myself, wrapped in my drug-induced blanket, staring at her thin frame and beaklike nose, that Zahava is a door. She is a bridge, a phone booth. Things would work out well if I stayed with her, I thought. She'd teach me how to be like her.

When we came home in the morning my body felt like cake batter and Zahava was complaining of canker sores. Her gums were patterned with pink-lined white squares and there was blood around her teeth. I hadn't been able to pee so I went to the bathroom. I stood in front of the bowl and waited. When I came out Zahava was staring at the wall with her hands on her hips, lightly biting at the inside of her mouth. Her stereo was gone, along with her music. "I hope they fry," she said this time. "Why not just kill all of them?"

"What do you mean?"

She looked at me like I knew what she was talking about and I shouldn't act stupid. She poked her chin forward and reconsidered. "I don't mean that. Really. I was just upset for a moment."

"I don't care about police," George says. He's getting anxious. I can't hold his attention. I'd think the ward would be unbearable for him, the small locked rooms, his eyes darting all over the walls.

"If you don't care about the police why do you tell them so much?"

He shrugs his shoulders and knits his brow. He has a low hairline that starts almost immediately above his eyebrows. "I don't know," he says, angrily, because he doesn't like that he's been tricked and he doesn't like that I'm telling him he's been tricked. It may be too late. He doesn't know his court date. Maybe it's already passed. They tried him, found him guilty, decided his fate, and he's sitting here waiting for it, waiting for it to come down on his neck like a mousetrap. And it will. They'll split him wide open. But even so. There are other mistakes to be made. No matter how much they pull you apart there's always room for another mistake, there's always something left.

"You think the police are your friends?" I ask him. "Is that why you tell them so much?" His eyes are really darting now and his legs are shaking and his thumb is beating the table. Sure, what's so hard about getting a confession from this kid? Leave him in a small room and wait for him to lose his mind. I stub my cigarette out. I feel almost dizzy, slightly nauseous. My tongue sticks and the roof of my mouth is thick and wet. There's a sharp pain in the back of my head wrapping itself around my ears like a steel belt and I press my palm against my forehead to relieve the pressure.

"No. I hate the police," he says.

The third time Zahava was robbed the robbers were caught. The landlady had drilled a wooden plank into the living room floor to keep the patio doors from opening. So they broke the window. It was daytime. The police were waiting for them or the neighbors had been put on alert and were watching. The robbers were ambushed or caught walking away. The police were called and they responded. "They always return," the police officer told us, standing in a pile of glass in the front room. "Creatures of habit. They catch themselves."

There were two robbers. An older man, past forty, a career criminal, just out of the can for the third time. And with him a young first-time offender named for a general who led his country against the English. And the child had a gun in his belt.

The burglars were taken to the Twenty-Fourth District police headquarters on Clark Street, a single-floor black metal building responsible for all of Rogers Park. There they were separated. I could trace their steps from the backseat of the car, a sun-filled parking lot shining with blue and white stripes, through the thick steel doors. I know what the room looked like where they sat the younger one and handcuffed his wrist to the loop in the wall. He was sitting on the bench between two desks, his hand raised like he was giving an oath. At one of the desks would be a plainclothes juvenile officer and a typewriter, and at the other a snarling blue jacket with horrendous skin and a tightly clipped brown beard. The bench would have been painted white for no discernible reason and bolted to the wall by two long chains. Next to the plainclothes would be the cell. The door to the cell would be open, offering a view of a clean steel cot and a toilet. And this is where young George Washington would spend the first night of his journey into the whirlwind.

First there would be questions. Legal counsel was not going to be an option. There was no right to remain silent. But maybe he wouldn't talk for a while. Not until the blue jacket punched his face a couple of times. Or maybe he would talk right away, while the juvenile officer typed. Because he doesn't care, because he's sure he's stronger than them and they can't do him any harm anyway so what does it matter. He's wrong about that. So they ask him if he was there all three times the apartment was robbed and he candidly responds yes. And they ask him if he had a gun on him then too. And he says yes. The police officers are nodding encouragement. He's getting excited. He's surging with his own invincibility. And then they tell him there were two people sleeping that first time they robbed the apartment. How did he

feel about that? He shrugs his shoulders. He doesn't feel anything about that. What if one of them had gotten up? What if
they had been discovered robbing the apartment? What then?
What would he have done if one of the occupants had come out
of the bedroom to see what all of the racket was or to use the
bathroom? What then? And George Washington pondered his
answer for a moment, growing stronger and nodding his head.
The air was rushing into his lungs. He was going to peel the roof
from the police station and pull the rest of it to the ground.
"I would have shot them dead," he replied.

"I'll go take a look."

"Don't bother. Stay here," she said, holding my hand.

"Well?"

"Well what?"

I think about asking for another cigarette but don't bother.
"The police," I say. I'm sweating but it's not hot in this room.
"Why did you tell them that?"

"Tell them what?"

"That you were going to shoot us. That you were going to
shoot the occupants of the bedroom if they walked out of the
room? You threw it all away. Why did you say that?"

"Doesn't matter."

"It does matter." I wish there was a window in this room or
less light but there isn't. "It matters," I say. "They're going to use
that against you. They put it in your report. They told the people
that live there you said that. They met them right outside of their
building and they said they had caught the robbers and that the
youth had a gun and he had intended to use it had they caught
him. That means for sure it's in your paperwork. And the prose-
cutor is going to present that to the judge. And you are never

going to get out. You are never going to go home again. You will be here until you're eighteen and possibly longer if they can figure a way. Because it's a different crime now. You've elevated the crime. You're no longer eligible for placement. Who can even imagine what they're going to call that, the places you're going to be. They're going to hold you until you're eighteen."

George's hair and eyebrows come together. He blows air into his cheeks. "Fuck you," he says.

"Fuck me? Fine. Fuck me. Don't talk to any more cops. You understand?" I realize that I'm shaking the table so I grip the table harder and shake it as hard as I can. "I don't care if they smack you with spoons, stick a hook in your penis, or what they threaten you with. You wait. Don't trust any of them. Not the teachers, not your guardian, or the guards or the lawyers. Definitely not the social workers or anyone who presents themselves to you as your therapist. That's a setup. They're out to get you. They fucking hate you."

He's crying now. I'm making him cry. "They are out for you. They don't give a shit about you. You're just food to them. They're going to eat you alive. And if a judge asks you, if you even get that chance, which you probably won't. But if you ever do, if the judge brings you into the courtroom. If a judge asks you if you were really there that first time and if you had a gun then you say no. You hear me? You say no. You say it wasn't even your gun. You were just carrying it for the other man. The *older* man. You were carrying it for him. It was his gun. Do you get that now?"

He's sitting upright. Tears are streaming from his hard eyes. The tears keep running, pouring over his cheeks, snot hanging from his nose, water dribbling over his chin, soaking the collar of his shirt, forming small puddles on the table. I sit and I wait. I can't let the guard see this. I have to be careful. I have to wait and then I have to go. I'll never make it out again. No one will protect me. I'm going to stand up and ring the bell and leave, let me out let me out, and that's the last I'm going to see of this place.

The stairs are long and empty. They never search you when you leave. I keep my hands just outside of my pockets. I walk the stairs and pass the guard and his metal detector. A funny thought occurs to me of putting a bomb together while inside and walking right out with it into the hot air and blowing up the rest of the world.

Western is twenty-three hundred west and eleven hundred south. Where I live is far north, east of the train tracks, near the lake and the suburbs, but not quite at either. I'll have to take three buses to get home. The heat attacks me. The exhaust sticks in thick grey streaks to the sides of white delivery trucks. As I'm walking away from the building my pace is quickening. I'm so afraid. I keep imagining that I was caught, even though I wasn't. It's like falling from a window. I'm walking faster, unbuttoning my shirt. Taking my shirt off, popping a button, wiping my face with my shirt. I'm running stripped to the waist. I'm running as fast as I can past the people waiting for a bus and the Payless shoe store. I'll yell. I'll get somewhere alone and I'll yell. I'm moving around the pedestrians, jumping into the gutter and then back onto the pavement.

"Ain't nobody chasing you," a man leaning next to a newspaper box yells after me. I stop and turn to look at him. He's a large man and his sweat has made his striped shirt transparent over his dark belly. He's laughing, turning a toothpick in his teeth, jingling some keys in his pocket. There's a wire garbage can nearby. A woman standing in the shade of a thin tree is turned slightly away from me, a smile playing beneath the dew of sweat on her lips.

CHAPTER SIX

STALKING GRACIE

It's 6:30 in the morning, and Maria is still asleep. I'm awake before the alarm goes off, but I don't move yet. Her back, with its thick pale scar, is pressed against my chest. I have to be careful when I get up. If I move too quickly, Maria will startle awake and want me to stay, and I can't miss another day of work. We can't afford that. I want to get inside her now, but I resist.

Our place is on the north side of Chicago, in an area known alternately as Rogers Park and the Jonquil Jungle. There are thirteen apartments on every floor. We live on the third floor, in a small room with a kitchenette, a half fridge, and one window, but we have our own bathroom. The paint in the hallways is dark red and cracked. The girls that work the sidewalk in front of the bookstore on Howard all live here, five or six to a room. They bring their customers in and out, and their customers come from everywhere. We've changed the locks on the door three times.

I raise the window shade to let in a little light and pull on my pants. I boil water in a saucepan, fill my coffee cup, two spoonfuls of instant coffee one spoonful of creamer, and sit at our table. We just moved in here when Maria turned eighteen. My caseworker told me they're replacing the furniture at the day center, so Maria and I might get a new table and some other stuff this weekend.

Maria sleeps naked on the mattress a few feet away. The blanket has slipped off her shoulder, and her breast is exposed. She looks as if she's having good dreams. This is rare. Normally the blanket is pulled tight around her shoulders, gripped in bunches. She sleeps with her eyes pressed shut and her mouth wide open, and she talks in her sleep.

I drink my coffee slowly and take one of Maria's paperbacks off the shelf. I read two sentences, then put it back. She's always reading. She likes romances. I told her she should write a romance about us, but she said nobody would be interested, because we don't have nice things. She reads while she's filling in at the branch library, and she summarizes the stories for me when I get home.

I take one last look at her before leaving to catch the 7:15 train. She'll wake up soon and call me at work. But now she's breathing easily.

"Most file clerks don't stick around," Ms. King says. "We have a high turnover because of the monotony." Ms. King wears her thick red hair in a tight ponytail. She has a small mouth and pointy teeth, and she questions the minutes on my timecard every week. She's thirty years older than me and was once married, but now lives alone in an apartment in Lincoln Park, not far from the zoo.

"You don't have to worry about me leaving," I tell her. "I'm not going anywhere."

I'm working on benefits for overseas employees. The rows of filing cabinets are endless: half a floor of a building downtown. I work slowly but steadily under the long fluorescents, organizing the folders by location, then specialty, then last name. The file cabinets are in the middle of the building, far from the windows, and are ringed by offices that nobody uses. On each office door there is a nameplate and a white board and a marker for leaving messages. Occasionally, when no one is looking, I'll write a joke message on someone's door.

I read through the enormous sums of money, salary, compensation, and per diems the overseas employees receive. They all come from good schools; it says so on their résumés, attached to the files. The receptionists keep plates full of apples on their desks. The advertising firm consults for governments. It has copywriters stationed in China writing political billboard ads.

Ms. King tells me I have a phone call.

"When are you going to be home?" Maria asks.

"You know already. It's all the way out there by the western suburbs. The brown line stops running after seven. I'll have to come back through downtown."

"I never should have encouraged you."

"You were trying to be supportive. After today I'll be home every day by six."

"I'm not going in to work today," Maria says. "I'm going to see Jackie instead."

Jackie is Maria's therapist. When you turn eighteen, as Maria and I both did recently, you lose your status as a ward of the court, but you still have access to social services for a year. If you're good, the state will even pitch in on your rent.

"Don't tell her about Gracie, OK?" I say.

"Jackie thinks you should be in therapy too. You're more messed up than I am."

"I hope not."

"I could get in trouble if you get caught," Maria says. "I could lose my privileges. I need my therapy."

I can picture her holding the phone against her ear with her shoulder and squeezing her arms together. Ms. King is standing at her desk, watching me.

"Theo?" Maria says.

"Yes?"

"I wish when you left for work that you would tie me up like a pig. You could use the electrical cord. I'd have to wait here for you like that."

Ms. King brushes past me.

"I want you to hit me so hard I have bruises everywhere," Maria says. "You don't hurt me enough."

"Tell Jackie about that."

"I can't. She'll think I'm a slut."

"I've got to get back to work."

Maria's sigh comes through clearly over the phone.

Before I leave work, I finish organizing all the employees in Japan. Ms. King asks me if I would like to contribute to the bagel pool. Everybody pitches in two dollars, and on Fridays we have bagels and cream cheese.

"But I'm a temp," I tell her.

"But you eat the bagels, don't you?"

"I'll have to talk to the agency about that."

"You know, Theo, you shouldn't be on the phone so much at work."

Mr. Gracie is a security guard at the Standard Oil Building. I saw him again for the first time a little over a month ago, while I was walking to the beach on my lunch break. I recognized him immediately. I stopped on the sidewalk, and people had to walk around me.

I wait for him today after work, as I have every weekday for the past month. I watch him pull his coat from a hidden closet behind the security desk, tip his hat to the man arriving for the next shift, and push through the revolving doors to the subway line. I follow him to the train, keeping a few people between us. I shouldn't be wearing a jacket in this hot weather, but I am. A light blue denim with an inside pocket.

I'm hoping he doesn't apologize. If he apologizes, I don't know what I'll do.

We take the underground pedestrian tunnel between the two main subway arteries of the city; the long corridor amplifies the sound of the commuters' footsteps. I swear I can smell his cologne. The traffic in the tunnel runs both ways. I push against people and walls trying to get through.

Mr. Gracie gets on at the front of the car, and I get on in the back. The blue line hurtles toward the Kennedy Expressway and the northwest suburbs, out by O'Hare. He sits on the outside of a two-seat bench. No one sits next to him.

When I first saw Mr. Gracie, I was surprised that he didn't look very different: the same short black stubble on his chin, top two buttons open on his shirt. But then, it's only been a few years. People don't change that much when they're in their forties. I look different. I have long hair now. In the juvenile center they kept it cut close to the scalp. My hair is straight and blond and hangs past my collar. This could be one reason Mr. Gracie hasn't noticed me following him. Another might be that he isn't looking. A third might be that there were so many boys he can't remember us all.

We pass Fullerton and the barrio. The Polish restaurants and the Ukrainian Village. I tug on my jacket, adjust the weight in the pocket. He's just sitting there.

A few weeks ago, on a Saturday, Maria and I went on a picnic with our friends Dave and Nadia. Nadia's pregnant, and Maria rubbed her face against Nadia's belly and put her hands inside the waistband of Nadia's shorts, on her stomach.

"Babies," Dave said, handing me a paper plate with a tuna sandwich and potato salad on it. "Who gives a fuck about babies?" He laughed.

I took a seat next to Maria. She didn't want to eat. She didn't want to move away from Nadia's stomach.

Maria's the smartest person I've ever met, but she had a hard time getting through the system. She taught me multiplication and has won every game of backgammon we've ever played; she always locks up my last five spaces. She carefully explains every move, but I never get it. I'm smarter than her in one way, though: I know every major street in Chicago and the address numbers of each block. I knew the boundaries of all the neighborhoods by the time I was thirteen.

At Foster, a Chicago Transit Authority officer boards the train and stands next to where I'm sitting, his holstered pistol inches from my nose. He's scowling and his hand drops heavily over the gun, his fingers pressing the leather.

The third time I followed Mr. Gracie home, I hid in his neighbor's bushes across the street. I thought someone had seen me, so I crouched quietly in the dirt and waited. I felt as if I were naked and hiding in the bushes so that nobody would see me without my clothes on, like in a dream. I crossed my arms over my chest. I thought the police were going to come and surround me and ask what I was doing, and I was going to have to admit that I was following Mr. Gracie. They would grab me by the arm and ask why. They'd laugh at my nakedness. They'd want reasons, but I wouldn't have any to give them. When I run through this in my mind, I shake my head slowly and also kind of nod knowingly at the same time. I say to myself repeatedly, *I am following Mr. Gracie.*

Nobody saw me behind the neighbor's bushes, and I hid out there and watched him come home and waited for the lights to snap on. I learned that he has a wife and two children, a boy and a girl. They live in a bungalow in Jefferson Park. After eight they sit together in the living room and watch television. He has children. That kills me.

When I first started coming home late, Maria thought I was cheating on her. She broke all our dishes. Standing in the mess she'd made, I told her that I had seen Mr. Gracie and I had been following him. She knew who Mr. Gracie was and what had happened between him and me. At first she was interested. She'd be waiting at the table when I got home. "What did he do today?" she'd ask. "Eat an apple? Read the newspaper?" Sometimes Maria would have bruises or a bloody lip. "I tried to wait for you, but it got late, so I had to go out." Yesterday she told me I had to finish the job, or she was going out and not coming home again. For Maria, being alone is the hardest thing.

Mr. Gracie unzips his bag and looks inside. Satisfied, he zips it back up. The CTA officer exits the train, hand still massaging his gun holster, and looks both ways in the station.

In juvenile, none of us knew anything about the staff's outside lives. We didn't even know their first names. The staff carried nightsticks and handcuffs. We had baggy brown pants and T-shirts. I had been in a glass cage for two days when Mr. Gracie came to get me. He told me to walk close to the red lines on the floor. Western was dark, and everyone's gym shoes were out in the hallway, their doors locked from the outside. Mr. Gracie took me into an empty office. He told me to put my stuff in the corner.

"You think you're tough?" he said. "You like to fight? You want to fight me?"

He stood a foot taller than me, but he was thin. His arms were like reeds. He slapped me hard and quick across my cheek. I knew better than to try to cover myself. Then he strip-searched me and made me do squats while he pressed on my shoulder. He told me to stand up and place my hands behind my head, and he poked at my ribs, flicking his middle finger hard. Then he bent me over the steel table and raped me, occasionally hitting my face, his hand flying out from some unseen place behind me. When he was done, he took me back to my room.

In a perfect world I could sit alone with Mr. Gracie and ask him questions, and he would tell me the truth. Maybe we would have a drink, a beer or coffee or something. We'd have time to spare. I picture us sitting on a bed, fully clothed, in a cheap hotel.

The first thing I would ask him is how he lost his job. Did he get caught? I don't think he got caught, because I don't see how he could get a job as a security guard at the fifth-largest building in the world if they had caught him. They could have just suspected something, or maybe they made a deal. But I don't think so.

Then I would ask him how he met his wife. Did he know her when they were young? What kind of games do his children play and does he worry about who's watching them when he's not around? I'd like to tell him about Maria, about her uncles and her grandmother. How she masturbates until the insides of her thighs are black and blue, and I masturbate with her until the skin on my penis breaks. How she calls me at work crying, saying she's been shoving the vacuum cleaner between her legs, and she's hurting. How, once, because I had done something wrong, Maria whipped me across the face with her belt. I got down in front of her and held her legs. She yanked on my hair with both hands and yelled, "You're worthless!"

The next night I brought her flowers. I was hoping she would hit me again, call me names, tell me how worthless I am. I rushed home from work every day, hoping. But she wouldn't do it, not even when I asked. That's when she really started cheating on me. She said whipping me made her feel bad about herself. She wanted to be abused. But I wanted the same thing.

"I'm starting to hate you," Maria said. "I want you to hit me, and you want me to hit you. This is terrible."

She went out nights. She met a man with a red beard who held a knife beneath her nipple and dared her to move. She got into cars with strangers. A man stuck a screwdriver in her ass. After a week of this, I started hitting her again, because it keeps her home and safe. When she goes out looking, walking down to the gas station late at night in her underwear, anything can happen. Somebody's going to kill her someday. I'd like to tell Mr. Gracie about Maria. I'd like to ask Mr. Gracie for his advice. What should I do?

When the train stops at Belmont and Kimball, a large crowd of people get off, and Mr. Gracie and I look at each other. Our eyes meet. The Belmont and Kimball station is underground and curved like a missile silo, only made out of brick. I'm being careless today, which is why Mr. Gracie has seen me. But he looks away. He pulls a newspaper out of his bag, opens it, and begins to read.

He would come and get me about once a week; I never knew exactly when. I'd wait in my room for him. I remember Mr. Gracie's hands closing around my neck, how I couldn't breathe, and then how I didn't want to breathe. I remember how his body felt warm on my back and how, when he pulled away from me, I felt exposed, as if somebody had yanked a blanket off me.

I remember what Mr. Gracie said to Larry, after he knocked Larry in the teeth with his billy club: he said that if anything happened to me, he was going to hold Larry personally responsible. That if I so much as cut my finger, Larry was going into the hole. Larry, the biggest kid I've ever seen, with biceps like watermelons. And I remember the look of fear on that kid's face. And my fear, hoping I would be gone before Mr. Gracie, because after Mr. Gracie there would be no one to protect me. But I wasn't—he left first.

Jefferson Park is the last stop in the city. I follow Mr. Gracie off the train. We walk down the iron stairs to the bus terminal. The air reeks of gasoline. People are milling around, and ten buses are waiting to haul passengers to Cicero, Berwyn, Rosemont, and points west. I lose Mr. Gracie for a moment in the crowd, but then I find him again, negotiating his way around a large woman with a stroller. He strides up the steps onto the Archer 68 bus. We're a long way from downtown. Mr. Gracie's commute takes more than an hour.

I sit right across from Mr. Gracie. I put my hand over the pocket of my jacket. I'm doing this for Maria. He puts his paper down on the seat next to him, it unrolls to the classifieds, and we look each other straight in the eye. He's wearing a light cloth jacket. He still has broad shoulders, but he looks thin now, almost frail. Suddenly I feel panicked. It's a hot summer day, but the air conditioning on the bus is turned up too high. A minute ago I felt the heat crawling below my skin. Now I feel cold and stiff.

"So," Mr. Gracie says, rolling the word around in his mouth like a gumball. "What's on your mind?"

I try to smile. I place my hands on my knees. Mr. Gracie places his hands on his knees as well. Mr. Gracie has long, thin legs. He looks like a spider.

"I'm glad you're not working there anymore," I say. "You're a predator."

"A predator," Mr. Gracie says, and he lets out a small laugh. He takes a cigarette from his pocket and slides the window open.

"No smoking on the bus," the driver says, looking in his rearview mirror.

For all the people in the station, the bus is sparsely occupied, eight or nine passengers. Archer is a desolate street: closed-down factories, hot-dog stands. It runs on a diagonal through the West Side. The street itself makes no sense in the city's layout, as it never reaches downtown. Mr. Gracie shrugs his shoulders, kicks one leg over the other, leans back. I watch his face for signs of fear. If only I could get Maria to understand me more. She always does what she wants.

"Terrible," Mr. Gracie says, craning his neck to catch a glimpse of the world outside, "to work so hard all day and step out into this kind of heat. I've always worked hard for less than I'm worth."

I start to look away but catch myself. I want to be aggressive. "You know what you did."

Mr. Gracie narrows his vision on me, letting the outside world pass by unnoticed. "How about this," he says. It's a familiar tone of voice, and I slip back, pressing my tailbone against the seat. "If you still had anything left to you, which you don't, I'd do it again." I can see his teeth. "Look at you. Look at how you're dressed." I look at my old jacket, my only pair of work pants. Why can't I have nicer clothes? "You look like an old man. You should at least have learned how to dress. Don't you have an iron?"

I look down at the floor, fold my hands. My script is gone. I had it planned out, everything, but now it's gone, gone. I try to think about his wife and children, but I can't. My mind doesn't want to think. I can't bring up the images. I can't remember what it looked like but my memory is just dull yellow paint and a thin strip of metal at the end of an office shelf. I shake my head.

The floor of the bus is polished steel, with thick ridges that run from the door to the back window. There were no windows in the detention center, and the windows in the group homes were webbed with wire.

We ride for miles in silence. Just before Mr. Gracie gets off, he says to me, "That's a big city out there. Eat a man alive." He pauses. "Somebody should have taken you home, you know?" He stands in front of me and places his hand, his long fingers, over my face, his palm resting on my jawbone, his fingers over my eyes and across my forehead, his thumb in my ear. "Do this for me: Get a haircut. Clean yourself up a little. You'll feel better about yourself."

He starts to move his hand, but I press my face against it, pushing into his palm.

"Don't follow me anymore, Theo. I can't take care of you. I have my own family. You wanted to have this talk. Fine. Remember, I kept you safe. You were safe when I was around. None of those boys did anything to you when I was there. You know why I kept you safe, right?"

I nod my head.

"That's right. But you're on your own now. Take care of yourself." Mr. Gracie pulls his hand away, slaps my knee with the paper. I hear the squeak of the bus door opening. The sound of boots in a hallway.

By the time I step into the apartment, it's late. The orange glow of the streetlights filters in around the drawn window shade. I'm relieved when I hear Maria's breathing. Then I see the dark blue handprint on her shoulder. She's lying in bed, staring at me. I peel my clothes off, fold them carefully into the milk crates, hang my jacket in the closet. In the bathroom I run the water and wait for it to get hot, then soak a towel with hot water and hold it against my face. I shave carefully with soap and my old razor. I cut myself only once. Then I pull the razor blade out and make a tiny cut on my shoulder. A thin, stinging cut. There's hardly a drop of blood. Then I cut myself three times more, making a little tick-tack-toe board on my arm. I run my finger over the wound, push gently to make it hurt. Lean forward into the wall and push harder. Breathe in the tiles and the mildew, the smell of the sink. Breathe.

I climb onto the mattress with Maria. She's wearing scented lotion.

"Did you do it?" she asks.

She's a silhouette. The sound of transactions on the street below filters through the window. We can always hear the noise from the streets. It's one of the many reasons why the rent is so low.

"We talked," I say.

She turns to me. Her soft arms and the web of veins running from her elbows. Her unshaven armpits. "That's not what you said you were going to do."

"I wanted to."

She turns away from me, tucks her hands beneath her head. It's gotten very late.

"Don't turn away from me," I say, grabbing her hair tightly. She lets out a gasp and carefully backs her warm body into mine.

CHAPTER SEVEN

WHERE YOU COULD END

THE SIGN READS *No Parking First and Third Tuesday November thru April*. I'm standing next to a newspaper box holding the pole. A police car drives past me, its wheels lifting and sliding on the ice before disappearing beyond the Pita House and the video store.

The roads are covered in salt. I've been staying with my friend Jackson and I'm wearing his large red flannel jacket with the blue padding inside. I'm hoping he lets me keep it. It's a comfortable jacket and I'd freeze otherwise. The wind is blowing. In the winter the wind-chill is the only measure that matters. I wish Maria would get here before the cold moves into me permanently.

She approaches from the alleyway watching the ground and then looking up and waving. Maria wears blue leg-warmers and gloves with the fingers cut. She walks with her feet pointed away, like a duck. Back at her home she has a poster of Madonna over her bed, lying in a wedding dress, "Like a Virgin" written along the top. This is a dangerous spot for me, the girls' group home just a block away. The staff there would recognize me, then call people who would force me into a car and take me somewhere, I'm not sure where. I'm not sure what they'd do. They'd lock me back in Reed and dope me full of Thorazine and sit me on a plastic couch in front of a television. Or they'd put me in Central Youth Shelter, thirty of us on mattresses on the floors. Gladiator arenas. Cut your face, cut your neck, steal your shoes. Hide in the corners, keep watch on all sides.

Maria stops before the newspaper box and I come forward to meet her, draping myself across her shoulders and melting into her collarbone. I feel her arms searching my ribs. "Dodo head, it's cold out here," she says.

"I should have checked the weather report this morning."

We sit in a booth at the back of the restaurant with a jug of coffee between us. "Do you want something to eat?" I ask. There's a family at a table near the center of the restaurant, a large man and his two small children drawing on the table with crayons. I'm still shivering a little and trying to smoke my cigarette. I look across my shoulder to the parking lot. Lincoln Avenue ends at Lincoln Village, the last strip mall before the suburbs. All along Lincoln are the places we're too young to go in, bars and truck stop motels. When I was eleven a man offered me $10 and took me to a hotel room on Lincoln. There was supposed to be a woman there, but there wasn't. Nothing much happened. The men that were there, the ones with the money, the one in the nurse's outfit, wanted a black boy, not a white boy, so they let me go.

"I'm not eating," Maria says. "I'm trying to lose weight."

The waitress tucks her pad into her apron, pulling the straps tight around her hips. "One hour time limit. Don't forget."

"Listen," I say to Maria. "A man goes to the doctor and he says, 'Doctor, I've got this problem, I'm in love with my horse.'

And the doctor says, 'Well, is it a male or a female?' And the guy says, 'It's a female. What, do you think, I'm queer or something?'"

Maria snorts and shakes her head at me. "Joker. You have to go back," she says. "You're going to get staffed out." I've been gone eight days. After fourteen days it's the policy of all state homes to staff the children out. Once you're staffed out you can never get back in.

"I failed my drug test," I tell her, dumping a creamer into my coffee and sticking my spoon into the cup. I lift the cup with both hands and hold it in front of my face like my father used to.

"Gee, how do you think that happened?" she asks.

"They're going to ship me to Prairie View for rehab."

Maria doesn't say anything. She lives in Peterson, a converted three-flat for girls who weren't adoptable. People joke that Peterson is a two-abortion home; girls with three abortions are sent somewhere worse. Every kid in the homes knows the different facilities you can be sent to. Prairie View is in the middle of the woods near the border with Wisconsin. There's no getting out. The first week they lock you in a time-out room with a glass door and push food through the slot in the morning. You're not allowed to talk to anybody. After that they come and ask if you're ready to join the program. They leave you in the cage until you say yes sir or ma'am. Once in Prairie View you stay until you're eighteen.

"Do you think I could have a tomato juice?" Maria asks.

I try to get the waitress's attention.

"Waitresses don't like to wait on Mexicans," she says. "They think we should be in the kitchen or bussing tables."

"If I go to Prairie View I'll never see you again."

Maria thinks it over. "You only have a year and a half left. Then we'll be eighteen and we can live wherever we want."

"Would you cook for me?" I ask.

"I'm not a very good cook."

"What kind of apartment should we get?"

"A big two-bedroom in a nice neighborhood." Maria drinks her coffee black. "Paula's been stealing my socks."

"Why?"

"She says she doesn't want to do laundry. She said if I tell anybody she'll pull all my hair out." Maria puts her coffee down and looks at the bus stand where an old man with a white sack is gripping the rail, trying to pull himself onto the first step. Maria leans forward over the table. "On the news last night they found two people frozen on Lower Wacker Drive."

"Since when do you watch the news? You don't know that." I pull the twenty-dollar bill Jackson gave me and lay it on top of the tab. "In Prairie View you're not allowed to make phone calls. There's no such thing as visitors. If you get angry the staff comes up behind you and pulls a paper bag over your head with a smiley face painted on it."

A grin spreads across Maria's cheeks. "Could be an improvement," she says. Whatever I say she's always two answers ahead of me. "You have to go back. Look at it out there." She cups her mug in both hands like me, the steam rising through her hair.

There's an alarm going off. Julie hurries from the bedroom into the bathroom, her shifting robe exposing her long pale legs. I think I see a white breast exposed in the open cloth. I sit up on the couch and rub my face. The alarm is still ringing, like a bell whistle. Then a bump, plastic breaking, and the alarm stops. It's snowing. Across the way are enormous Section Eight tenements, windows ringed with black ash from old fires, the ledges now covered in snow.

Jackson comes out of the bedroom buttoning the top of his jeans. Jackson's got a face full of lumps and looks like he's smiling even when he's not. He looks like he got hit with a sack full of quarters. "You ready to make some money today?" he asks, standing in the hallway, waiting for his wife to come out of the bathroom.

"We have to sit in the back of the truck?"

Jackson sees beyond me, the snow falling in the backdrop. "Oh shit," he says, rapping his knuckles against the bathroom door, then smacking the door with his open palm twice. "Get the fuck out of there already. Let's go."

I first met Jackson and Julie near the end of summer at Julie's brother's house, just across the street from the new group home I had been moved to. Jackson, Julie, and Jon were standing in front of the construction truck, drinking. I was just getting home from school and I stopped in front of them and nodded toward the paper bag near the stairwell with cans of beer in it. "Can I have one of those?" I asked. They looked at me like I was crazy. Julie smiled.

"Give the kid a beer," she said. "It's hot."

Later, inside Jon's place, Jackson jerked his head toward the window, where we could see the group home across the street. "You live in that place?" he asked. Julie was dividing up lines of PCP. "You don't have any parents?"

"We should adopt him," Julie said. I moved closer to her. She saw what I was doing and turned and blew smoke in my face.

"Put him to work on the truck," Jackson said. Everybody laughed, even me. They were pretty surprised when I showed up at their apartment three months later.

Mr. Berry, Julie's father, drives the small white construction truck. It's seven o'clock when we arrive at an old bungalow near

Sauganash. "Gonna be a quick day," the old man says.

Jackson surveys the house, his gloves on his hips. It's snowing steadily. "We'll just set a chicken ladder," Jackson says.

"Won't the ladder slide off the roof?" I ask.

"You want to work or not?" Mr. Berry asks impatiently. "I can take you home right now. Go on welfare like the rest of the fucking niggers."

"I didn't say that."

"It's called a chicken ladder for a reason, Theo," Jackson says. "It's for chickens. Chicken chicken chicken, *beowk*. 'Sides, it's not snowing that hard."

"This is nothing," Mr. Berry says. "Pigeon shit."

We haul the sand and concrete mix from the truck. The barrow, hawks and slicks, buckets, roofing, tools. When we've got everything the old man gives a hard wave and takes off. Jackson lights a joint and hands it to me.

"What are you going to do about school?" Jackson asks. He's concerned in the mornings. I take a hit off the joint and hand it back to him.

"Nothing," I say.

"You want to end up like me?" Jackson asks. "I guess that's not such a bad option." He pinches the lit top of the joint and drops it in his pocket.

I mix the cement while Jackson sets ladders. We each take a slop on our hawks and go to opposite sides of the house. To climb the ladders we lay the slick in the porridge and pull up with one hand. The first time I go my hand slides off and I feel a splinter lodge itself through my gloves. I lean my body into the ladder and try again. Eventually I forget the snow. There's nothing else to do but cut the cement and paint it onto the cracks in the house, wiping the excess from the bricks until my gloves weigh ten pounds. I've been told by Mr. Berry and Jackson that if you don't tuckpoint your house the house falls down. But Mr. Berry lives in an apartment. The old people in Sauganash certainly believe it; we come out here almost every day.

It's six at night and already dark when Mr. Berry comes to take us home. In the front of the truck, the heater blasting, crushed together, I'm trying to bite the splinter from my finger without banging my knee into the stick shift. I want to mention the short day but we're not even done yet. We still have to rinse out the cement and wash the side of the truck. "Took a loss on this one, boys," Mr. Berry says. "Have a better day tomorrow."

"This is all he gave you?" Julie asks, steering the light blue Chrysler from the side streets and onto the main road. "What did you do all day?"

"Tuckpointing," Jackson says, lighting a cigarette and handing it back to me. "The kid here did a good job today. There might be hope for him. It's too early to tell."

Julie reaches to the dashboard for her own cigarettes. "Give me what you have," she says, stretching her arm across the seat and tickling the bottom of my nose. I press my fifteen dollars into her palm. We drive the Lebaron down the length of Western Avenue to Humboldt Park and the buildings there; Mexico City, it's called. The snow is getting heavier and the wheels part the slush toward the sewer vents. While we drive we sing the theme song from *Sesame Street*, shaking our arms and shoulders like muppets.

I figure that with the weather so bad and the snow so heavy the store will be closed, which shows what I know. The man who's always been there, standing on this street in a big round black jacket, approaches the car. Julie rolls down the window for him and he sticks his head into the vehicle, his hat pulled over his eyes and piles of snow in the stitching. "Go slow," he says. "Police came through half an hour ago." He cranes his head in the car and looks through the front window down the stretch. "You got anything for me?" He makes a small twitching motion.

"Hard day," Julie says, smiling as much as she can but it doesn't come easy to her and it looks like it's going to tear her face. Snow falls in the car where the man's shoulders don't block the doorframe.

"Well that's different, holmes. That's different." He pulls his body back yet still manages to be inside the car, his hands digging in his jacket pockets. Snow falls in a curtain past his face. "I don't see how I can let you through. Not with the weather like this."

"C'mon," Julie says, flakes settling on her wrist. "It's a bad night. Tomorrow we'll bring something for you."

"Yeah. Tomorrow. Where is that? Is that in the phone book? I'm having a hard night too. Look at this shit."

"Oh fuck!" Julie says, smacking her palms on the steering wheel, her hands scrambling through her jacket like mice. She pulls out a five-dollar bill and thrusts it at him. "Fucking take it then."

"OK," he says. "OK. Take it easy." He stands half a foot away from the car, tucking the money inside his sleeve and briefly looking around the street. "We're all friends here. Let's have a good time, make it an easy night. Right? Drive slow. Don't freak anybody out."

Julie pulls over near the Z Frank car dealership and lays three lines on the dashboard, one noticeably smaller than the other two. The dealership light blinks on and off, sending waves of pink through the car. The pink highlights the veins in Julie's long neck and Jackson's apelike features. "You're too young. You don't want to get hooked on this shit," Julie says, doing her line first, then handing it to Jackson. I have to climb up front to do mine, hanging with my ribs over the chairback. Jackson hands me his half straw. I try to remember which side he used, then snort it up anyway. The PCP burns. It feels like soap and rocks tumbling down the back of my throat, and it takes a little while before I get that cloudy feeling and things start to haze over.

"Fucking Mexicans," Julie says, remembering her $5. "You'd think they'd be happy we let them into the country. We need to close the fucking border."

"My girlfriend's Mexican," I say and Julie looks back at me, both of her hands clutching the wheel. Her face is like a cinderblock. Her lips roll over her gums, bright red daggers splitting her teeth, then it passes and her features soften.

"That's too bad," she says, water rising to her pupils. "Too bad you have a girlfriend." Julie smacks her lips. "Because I have a friend, don't I, Jackson? Tracy. Yeah. She's got a great ass. You would love her ass. I told her we have a sixteen-year-old virgin sleeping on our couch. A little runaway, I said. And you know what she said? She's twenty years old and when I told her you sleep in your jeans she was like, Oooh, I like virgins. She seemed really excited. I was going to invite her over tonight to listen to some music and party. But I guess I won't. Unless you want me to. But if you have a girlfriend..."

"Do whatever you want," I say, my cheeks twitching. Jackson lets out one short, loud laugh.

"You've got a lot to learn, bro."

"Just like the rest of them," Julie says, jumping the car into gear. "So much for the innocent."

* * *

The blanket is wrapped around me and I'm cross-legged on the couch listening to the buzz of the phone on the other side. All of the doors in the apartment are closed. "Hello?"

"Maria?"

"Are you drunk?"

"A little bit." Julie and Jackson are in their bedroom now. They left an album playing on the stereo.

"What's that music?"

"That's Elvis."

"Oh. You shouldn't call so late over here. It's almost midnight. You'll get me in trouble."

"Sorry. We're getting up early again tomorrow." Out of the window it seems the snow has stopped. The city is covered with thick yards of white. I hear a crash behind her voice. "What was that?"

"Tamara and Jodie are fighting. I can't stand it." I picture Maria standing in the phone room, shaking her head, and the other girls breaking dishes and screaming just outside. Jodie is private and Tamara is a street fighter. I see Tamara pulling Jodie along by her hair, a dog on a leash.

"I wish you were here," I say. I hold the line, keeping my eye on the door to the bedroom. Maria doesn't say anything. "I wanted to hear your voice."

"Here I am."

"I'm going to take care of you."

"Ha ha. Now I know you're drunk."

"I mean it."

"What else do you mean?"

When Maria came to the boys' home the first time, I pretended not to notice her. One time she asked me to walk her to the store and all the boys laughed and whistled. After that we always split apart from everyone else. Maria would tell me why the state took custody of her. She told me about her grandmother letting her uncle rape her, how her uncle left her tied up overnight. She told me stories like I had never heard before.

"Maria, Maria, Maria." I wish I could sit behind her now, and comb her hair, and wrap my arms over her chest and my legs around her waist.

I see the door open.

"I have to go."

"Are you coming back? You only have a few days left."

"No," I say. "I can't."

Today we lay a roof on top of a split-level smoker in Edgewater near the hospital. Jackson and I join Julie's brother Jon and another crew with a tar heater. "Jon got a line on some dinosaurs," Jon says. He likes to talk about himself like he's not there. "Think about it. Jon Berry. Dinosaurs. Four o'clock." We shovel the steaming tar from the furnace onto the black top and spread it over the roof with mops. The sun is out and the air is dry and cold. Pushing a mop full of tar is like trying to shove a piano. The heat from the tar keeps us warm and some of us strip down to T-shirts. The men who lay roof all the time wear green shirts that read Harry's Roofers. They look like monsters from the movie *The Time Machine*, but without the fur. Their heads shaved, yellow eyes, tattoos running up their necks. By the time we finish my jeans are covered in tar stains.

"That will never come off," Jackson says to me.

"That's OK," I nod. "Now I have work pants."

"Do you have any other pants?"

"No. But I'll get some."

Jackson slaps my back. It's cold still but the sun is out now and the sky over Chicago is blue. The Sears Tower pokes above downtown, miles away, near the lakefront. Our breath escapes us in thick clouds and we stare at the sticky, shiny black top of this building and compare it with the dusty tops of the two-flats nearby. The other men stand across from us, also staring at the craftsmanship spread out before them. The day is over already. We worked through another one. The roof is a wonder to behold.

No one will ever find me. I am a phantom. Jackson and I smoke cigarettes with Jon and roll dice in the valley between the couch and the television set. Dinosaurs are actually Placidals, heavy-duty downers, big white horsepills twice as thick as a cigarette filter. I had to cut mine in half and take it in two swallows. We're all moving slow and the smoke swims through the air like fish. I am at the bottom of the world. Jon's pants are nearly falling off because he doesn't wear a belt. He leans forward on all fours on the floor, balancing on his elbow, mooning Jackson and me. He's blue from the smoke. Junky Smurf, I think to myself and nod my head. He's turning the dice over, matching them in his fingers, reminding me of the night I won the DCFS shirt and there was a fire in the group home. That was the best night of my life. "Keep drinking," Jackson says, shooting a ray with his pinky to the beer in front of me. "It'll help." Julie slams through the front door and beelines straight into the bedroom, leaving a long, dark trail behind her. Jackson's eyes follow her and rest heavily on the door.

"Watch closely," Jon says. Mr. Berry gave me $25 today, which means Jackson must have made forty. Jon puts the dice right up against his eye and stares into the center of the blocks. "Jon Berry needs a six," he says as the dice tumble over each other toward the bookcase. My lungs hurt and I cough. Mr. Berry asked me today how I liked laying roof. I said I liked it fine and he said that was good because Harry might want to hire me. Not enough work on the truck over the winter. Apparently roofers have a high turnover. Mr. Berry said roofers are only interested in making enough for their next fix.

Jon's dice come up eight. "Jon Berry needs a six," he says again, as if the dice had just misheard him the first time. Everything is very flat and on its side.

"Hold on a second. Just wait," Jackson says, getting up, then falling over the chair, tumbling headfirst into the wall, then crawling back to his seat and sitting back down again.

"Oh no," Jon says. "Watch Jon Berry."

The dice come up seven. We all look at the dice. Seven is a loser. The most losingest number of all time, unless you roll it first. I've never seen such a loser. Jon owes Jackson and me a dollar. What horrible luck. Unbelievable. How could anyone be so unlucky? It makes me sad. We watch the dice, waiting for them to make a move. "Boo," I whisper. Maybe they'll jump or something. If I concentrate hard enough the dice will fly around the room and roll for me. I can feel every piece of air in my nostrils, each molecule of oxygen. I can see a space three inches in front of my nose where nothing exists.

"You owe me a dollar," I say, because it's true. I am a speaker of truth.

"You'll get it," he says. "Absolutely. Double or nothing."

"Nope."

"Take it easy," Jackson says, waving his big hand in front of him, like he was clearing fog from a window and then closing his fist in front of his face, squeezing the sound from his fingers. "Everything's going to work out." I can't take it. I turn away from both of them. Outside it's starting to snow again. I think I'm going to cry. Things are not going to work out. It's going to be horrible. Look at all that snow, grabbing dirt from the sky and pulling it to the earth. Hiding it beneath the white surface. It's enormous, this city, it swallows everything. Maria lives out there in a building with bricks over the windows. She can't even see the snow that is hiding her. I bet she's staring at those bricks right now, wondering which side of them I'm on. I have to help her.

Nobody says anything for a long time. There's comfort in silence, and as the pills wear off Jon stands and leaves. His engine starting shakes the snow from the ledges. Jackson makes it into the bedroom. And I hear my name being called through the hallway and I follow my name to their door.

It's late, past midnight, and I'm freezing. Tiny icicles hang from my eyelashes and I can't do anything but keep moving and tighten my shoulders. Julie came in with some cocaine and we were all having a good time, I thought. The cocaine and the Placidal felt really good together. I came out of the fog. I told Julie and Jackson that I loved them. I told Jackson that he was my best friend in the whole world. I don't know if it was the buildup or the drugs. Jackson, Jon, and Julie had been swapping looks all night, like they knew something I didn't know. It was suspicious, now that I think about it. Then Jon left and it was Julie, Jackson, and me, and we were sitting on the bed in their bedroom. It's an enormous bed. It must be the biggest bed you can buy, and maybe even bigger than that. I can't even imagine how they got it in the room. And we were listening to the Rolling Stones at full volume. It was all breakdowns and missed opportunities. Then Jackson said I had to leave. And I said OK and got up to go to the living room. But he followed me.

"No, I mean it," he said.

"What do you mean?" I asked.

"You're going to get us in trouble." Jackson was jawing when he said it. I'd never seen him jaw before. He was grinding his teeth to dust and biting the tip of his tongue. "The cops are going to bust in. We're harboring a runaway." I looked at him and then the couch. I wanted to cry. Runaway is the wrong term. I've been labeled a runaway since I was eleven. "I mean you have got to get out of here." Then Julie stepped out and she was completely naked. I had never seen her naked before. She had a big tuft of red pubic hair fanning out over her thighs, and her legs and stomach were all flat muscle. But it was weird muscle, segmented in strange places. It wasn't round like I thought it would be. It was like her muscles were trying to get out of her skin and run away from each other. She stood behind Jackson, staring at me, her mouth wide open. Her eyes were solid black, all pupil.

"Can't I just spend the night? I'll leave in the morning."

Jackson was shaking his head and Julie grabbed onto his arm with both hands. I looked over Julie's strange body. Beneath her breast was a small blue tattoo of a bird flying. I didn't understand why Jackson had to be there at all. Why couldn't it just be me and Julie? I wanted so desperately to get into the bed with her and lie there. I wanted it with everything I had. I wondered what it tasted like between her legs and I thought about it so hard that my tongue grew thick. But I gathered my stuff together and put on Jackson's jacket. He didn't say anything about me taking his jacket. Then I walked out the door.

There's a row of mustard-colored three flats that run for a full city block between Pratt and North Shore. Some of the windows contain the flickering of television sets so I try to be careful and not walk under any street lamps. The cold is starting to hurt and I can't feel my ears. A man was following me for a while but it got too cold even for him and he quit. By the time I find the basement door I'm shivering hard and it takes three attempts, throwing myself at the door, to get it open. It finally buckles and breaks, the latch lying on a cement stairway leading into darkness, and as I stand and look at it the shapes become visible and the darkness disappears. I belong here.

The basement is empty save a few storage closets, a metal sink, and a washer-dryer. The floor and the stairs are painted blue. A single bulb hangs on a thick cord unlit in the center of the room. Rubber tubes covered in dust lie across the washing machine and over the sink. The dryer is clean, large, and sturdy. I start the dryer and it fills the basement with noise. I undress, peeling off my layers, and put my clothes in the dryer to heat them up. I cross my arms over my chest. I'm worried that someone will come into the basement and find me naked. Will they let me put my clothes back on or will I have to stay naked until I turn eighteen? I fold myself over the drying machine, rattling around on the blue floor. I hug it to try to quiet it down, my legs pressed against its front, and lay my cheek on the top, trying to get the heat to enter my body. The machine quivers, my clothes tossing inside of it. I stretch my arms to its back, feeling. There, the metal forms ridges like ribs that I slide my fingers between. I rub my face along the lid.

It's after school, and we're waiting for the car to arrive. The heat is on but I'm still shivering. Maria and I are holding hands in the smoking room. I've been waiting all day, putting my stuff together, watching television, smoking cigarettes. A staff member gave me a full pack as a going-away present. Maria only just got here. "At least I'll graduate high school," I say. "There's no missing classes in Prairie View. No point anyhow."

"You'll like school once you're into it," Maria says. Maria is the best student at CSC, the group home school. The CSC is just a holding pen, a babysitting facility. But her book is always open, no matter who's being restrained. She gets an A in every class.

I shrug. I don't want to talk about this. There's two staff members in the front of the house and we can hear other kids running up and down the stairs. There's windows looking into the empty play lot where I put up a basketball net last summer. We're being given alone time, Maria and I. They think they're generous, they all do. They think they're doing you a favor every time they leave you alone. I kiss her on the lips and slide my hand inside her sweater. She leans into me, resting her head on my shoulder. I run my finger along the edge of her bra and push under her breast. Her sighs are like music. I think of her grandmother selling her to support a heroin habit, the time she spent in the closet. I just want to protect Maria. I see her uncle breaking through the door night after night, Maria against the wall, biting at the piece of rubber she's been told to keep in her mouth, raped so many times the memories blur. I rub my fingers down her spine and she moves into me more and I pull her as she does. She lays her legs across my legs. We try to get inside each other. Soon the car will be here. "It won't be long," I say.

"No," Maria replies. "You'll be out soon."

You never know who's going to be in control of you once you're in a locked facility. And you never know what those people are going to do. When people are in control they're capable of anything. Adults are always waiting to attack and you have to do everything possible not to disturb them. They'll take you with their hand across your face. The car will be here any minute. It won't be so long. I kiss the top of Maria's head, the pale spot where her hair parts. Her hair is dry and sour smelling. I kiss her again. I will have years to keep her safe.

CHAPTER EIGHT

STEVENSON HOUSE

THERE ARE TWO yellow chairs, a green metal desk, and a round white clock on the wall.. Above the desk on a shelf are the staff logs, a row of diaries they keep on our daily activities. We're not allowed to read them. Yolanda's waiting for my answer. What was the question?

"How's school?"

"Same as last week."

We're in the staff office, a sheet of Plexiglas between us and the living room. Dante sleeps in the big chair, his fingers brushing the floor. Yolanda introduced him two weeks ago during dinner with her hand on the back of his collar. Something about, Let's make him feel at home. He's only thirteen, the youngest kid in Stevenson House. I'll be sixteen soon and will have a cake and a gift of my choice. Yolanda's only three years older than my roommate, Cateyes, who's eighteen and walking around the living room now on his hands.

"I have your report card," Yolanda says, though she isn't holding anything. Her hands are folded into her lap, she's wearing new nail polish, and she's staring at me and smiling. "I'm wondering how we can do better." She's wearing white tights. Her feet are crossed at the ankles. I can see little black hairs on her legs through the tights. She's too pretty to be staff here. "Theo?"

"I could go to class more."

"Yes ..."

All of the group home kids are wards of the court and we go to Kenmore, two miles east, close to the University of Chicago and away from the housing projects. There's a special school inside Kenmore, a school within a school, on the third floor, for kids with behavioral disorders, an automatic classification for us.

Cateyes doesn't have to go to school. He's a dropout. His feet are in the air, his shirt down around his chest, bunched at his chin, showing off the brand on his stomach, VL for Vice Lords. He says the El Rukns gave it to him when he took his orders. The scar is the color of a penny and sits a quarter inch over his muscles and the dark trail of short curly hair to his belt.

"You're not living up to your potential," Yolanda says.

Anybody in Stevenson who has perfect school attendance for a week gets four dollars. They pay us to go to school because there's only one staff in the morning and staff doesn't come to the second floor. So nobody wakes us up. Nobody makes us do anything. Second staff comes from ten in the morning to ten at night.

"I don't have any potential."

"Who told you that?"

She uncrosses and recrosses her legs, her skirt riding over her knee. Everybody meets with Yolanda once a week for one-on-one. And for an hour she pretends to care. Then she does it again with someone else.

"What I'm asking," she says, pulling her skirt down, "is how I could help."

"You could drive me to school in the morning." It's a joke but she seems to consider it. There's a loud bang. Cateyes is punching the Plexiglas.

"Watch this," he says loudly at the pane so we can hear him. Cateyes is the oldest resident in Stevenson House and he also wears glasses, much thicker than Yolanda's. Cateyes has a midnight curfew. For everybody else curfew is nine o'clock, except on bowling night. Cateyes throws his arms up, takes two steps from the window, and jumps, flipping over backward, landing on his feet. Yolanda claps her hands in appreciation.

"He's just trying to get your attention," I say.

"There's nothing wrong with that."

I shrug my shoulders and get up to leave. Our time is done for the week. Cateyes stops me on the way to the back door.

"What did she say about me?" he asks.

"She said you're a good acrobat."

"Damn right I am." I reach for the knob. "You better not be lying," he says.

"I'm not."

Kevin, Nettles, John, and Hunter are playing basketball behind the house. There's worse places than Stevenson House. Here, we come and go whenever we want and we have the only basketball court in the neighborhood. The hoop's even got a net.

Toby stands on the porch with a cigarette and offers it to me but I shake my head. Toby never plays, he just watches, his baseball cap pulled tight over his red curls. "Coming tonight?" he asks.

"Unless I get invited to some big party."

"You know something I don't?" He smokes his cigarette like it's a cigar, like he's celebrating, and I nod so he knows I'm joking and that I'll meet him in his room when everyone is asleep.

The court is surrounded by a fifteen-foot fence and beyond the fence a field filled with cinder blocks and patches of grass and then the first project building followed by rows of projects, to the horizon. The buildings are so tall that it's light outside hours after the sun sets behind them. Kevin has the ball and smiles like a lion. He's staff like Yolanda but he's been around longer. He only wears silk shirts and never takes his shirt off because he's a Muslim. Kevin is a gang leader for the Knights of Kaba. When he works nights he deals drugs out of the home.

"Larry Bird," he says, pointing to me. Nettles takes a frantic swipe at the ball and Kevin tosses it over Nettles's forearm, then catches it as if it were on a string. One time Kevin played against all eight of us and said he would buy us ice cream if we won. But we didn't because no one was willing to pass the ball. They're playing three on one, but Hunter and John seem stuck behind Nettles. Kevin rolls the ball around Nettles's waist. Nettles backs up, bumping Hunter. "Now," Kevin says. His feet shift and cross, the ball disappearing then reappearing again. Nettles jumps and lands just as Kevin leans back, his hands fading behind his head, his eyes closed. The ball catches softly in the net. Kevin looks around like he doesn't know where he is. "Ooooh. I'm good. Oooh oooh oooh." He walks on his toes with his hands bunched in front of him. "Ha ha. You ever seen anything like that, Theo?"

"No," I say from the porch, taking a drag from Toby's cigarette and handing it back to him. "I've never seen anyone walk like a hamster."

"Again," Nettles says. He's holding his hat in his left hand and running his right over his scalp.

"That's all right," John says, pulling up his pants. "We'll do it one net at a time."

"Don't ask me for shit," Hunter says. Hunter's big like John, but thick and solid. Hunter's dangerous because he's stupid and he's only your friend when he wants something. One time I went with Hunter to his home on the west side. Grown men recognized Hunter and moved out of his way. It was the afternoon and his mother greeted us in a transparent peach nightgown holding a glass full of ice. "Hello boys," she said. When she recognized us her expression changed and she told us to make some sandwiches.

"Go get your boys, big man," Kevin says, pretending to throw the ball at Hunter's head. Hunter puts his hands in front of his face. "Get 'em as big as they come so I can knock 'em down like bowling pins. Get in the game, Theo." He's holding the ball upside down in his palm. "Shoot it up, lightbulb." He bounces the ball to me at the free throw line. "North side, make it take it. First bucket for two."

"Lightbulb," Hunter laughs. "That's messed up."

"You do have a big head," John says to me.

"I'm going to pass you like the wind, fatso," I say. I turn the basketball over. I feel good. I'm going to have a good game. I hear the back door close as Toby goes back in the house.

"Don't hate me because I'm beautiful," John says.

"Shoot the ball already," Nettles says. "C'mon."

At night Cateyes leaves the radio playing beneath his pillow. His light snoring filters along the edges of the music, endless background noise, fast muffled house beats with repetitive lyrics: *it's not over, no it's not over, it's not over.* Occasionally I can hear a gunshot from the projects, or the fence rattling in the backyard. Sometimes I hear sirens, but usually the sirens are part of the song. If I reach below the pillow to turn the radio off Cateyes will wake up and I'll have to fight him.

Cateyes's small mustache catches bits of moonlight. He smiles when he sleeps and he never moves. I creep past his bed and out to the hall just as Dante is stepping from the bathroom. We stare at each other, then Dante disappears into his room.

I lock Toby's door behind me. Toby sits on his bed with his back to the window. He's not wearing socks or a shirt, and his torso is pale, freckled, and hairless. Ladders of scars rising from his shoulders to his elbows. He puts his thumbs up and I nod and give him two thumbs up.

"Hell yeah," he says, swinging his fists through the air.

"Keep it low," I say. "Dante's lurking."

Toby's last roommate got sent to Saint Charles, long-term, so Toby has a room to himself for a little while. The empty bed is stripped, the naked mattress faded with brown and red stains. Toby's room seems sparse and spacious with just him living in it, even though it just barely fits the two beds and dressers. He has an AC/DC poster and a *Friday the 13th* poster on the inside of the door, the killer in a hockey mask stalking forward. I sit down next to Toby; he bends his knees toward me. I pull the crumpled cellophane from my pocket while Toby lights a cigarette, takes a drag, and puts it in my mouth. "This rules," Toby says.

"Welcome to the windowpane." The windowpane is a red plastic tab with a silver lightning bolt jiggered unevenly across it.

"How do we do this?" Toby asks. I move away from him and grip the outside of the tab with my thumb and index finger and place it on the dresser. Toby stands, leaning against me, breathing on my neck.

"It's supposed to be the same as four hits. Got any scissors?"

"I have a knife." Toby digs his hand under his mattress and pulls out a large pocketknife with a wooden handle and a scrap of metal screwed into its end.

"Fuck," I say. "Who are you going to kill with this thing?"

"Your roommate," he says.

I pull the blade from the handle and it locks into place. I split the tab in half, digging the knife into the top of the dresser and leaving a big scratch that no one will ever notice. We each place a half under our tongue. I carve the anarchy A with a circle around it into the dresser.

"Once you kill someone you can never go back," I say, brushing the blade over my wrist and sucking on my cigarette as my skin breaks and a small drop of blood spills onto the floor.

"Cut yourself?" Toby asks.

"Just a little."

We smoke our cigarettes and wait. Then we light a couple more. Toby got a whole carton from somewhere. I stand against the dresser, then place my chin on top of the dresser in front of the knife and look into the grey piles of ash. Toby relaxes into his bed.

"Lay down," he says. "It feels good."

"I don't feel anything yet." The cigarette smoke is purple.

One night we took acid in Toby's room and couldn't figure out how to get the door back open. I climbed out his window and across the fire escape as if it were a monkey bar and swung through the window into my bedroom next door. Maybe I'll do that again. I like the way the stairs feel beneath my feet. You can use them for balance but if you try to put any weight on them they fall away from you. If I slipped I would have died but I felt like a superhero that night, two stories above the city, climbing in the air, the wind spearing through the towers, my feet against something unsteady. I could see the orange stripe of the hospital buried like a treasure inside the projects.

"There's a lot of people I want to kill," he says.

"Have you ever killed anyone?" I ask. I push the smoke from my mouth slowly so that it covers my face. I think of melting rain and buildings humming like speakers. I want to laugh.

Everything is so damn funny. I think of a city blanketed in fog, a horn sounding through the alleyways and long-nosed detectives in trench coats searching for clues. My father used to quote Humphrey Bogart. My father was killed with a shotgun at close range. My mother died shortly after that. She had multiple sclerosis and one day I came home late from school and her chin was on her chest, and I knew her head had fallen forward and she had been unable to breathe. I press my teeth together and my ears start to ring. It dawns on me that Toby probably has killed someone. Definitely Cateyes has, and Hunter. Hunter is big and dangerous. He once beat Cateyes to within an inch of his life and when Cateyes was lying unconscious Hunter kicked him in the back of his head. And Kevin, Kevin, Kevin, I'm sure Kevin's killed someone. I don't understand why Kevin even works here. I think Kevin is like Jesus. He's trying to teach us something. He said once he'd been at a college in California for a year on a basketball scholarship but had to return to the state. One time he asked me if I was high and I admitted I was and he gave me a piece of chicken that had been fried with honey inside of it. I've never tasted anything like it. He always has rolls of money in his pocket. When I asked him why he works here he just said that it was a good job for a thug.

Toby thinks about it for a second, like he's considering lying. Then he says no, he's never killed anyone. I wave my cigarette like a wand because I'm not sure if he chose to lie or not. I write my name in the air and try to inhale some of the smoke.

"You're my only friend," Toby says, staring into the ceiling, desperately squeezing his legs together and rubbing his hands over his pockets. "I cut myself with that knife before, a bunch of times. We're blood brothers. We need to back each other up."

"We need to not make any waves. I'm not your Tonto or Lone Ranger. I couldn't back you up if I tried."

"Let's go get my stepdad." He always wants to go find his stepfather on the north side. He blames his stepfather for his mother kicking him out of the house. After she kicked him out he burned down the Wheels Warehouse on Devon and they caught him and put him in the mental hospital. Then they discharged him here. People used to call him Crazy Toby, but it didn't really fit and people stopped calling him that.

I stretch my arms as far as they'll go. I feel like exercising. I wonder if I could exercise without moving. Toby's freckles are spreading like a red rash over his body. "What's happening to you?"

Toby's arms are wrapped around his knees. He looks like a beetle turned on his back. "You look like a clown," he says, the corners of his mouth dry and white. When he says something he leaves his mouth open. I had never realized before this moment that people always close their mouths after they say something. Everything's different. I take a deep breath and hold it for as long as I can, then release the air slowly. It feels like a finger rubbing my lungs. I do it again.

"I'm understanding things," I say. The walls are water. This must be what scuba diving is like. "I think I get it."

"You look like a killer clown. The kind that kills children. Going from home to home killing children. A psycho killer in a clown suit. Hey, clown killer."

"How can you tell without opening your eyes?" I light another cigarette and smoke two cigarettes at once then put the smaller one out, pushing it into the tray and studying the broken paper and last weeds of tobacco inside the ash. I hold my cigarette as close as I can to my hand without burning myself. Toby relaxes his legs and lays flat on the bed. He's serene and perfectly still. "I'll kill you," I say, crawling over him, next to the wall, stretching my mouth and twisting my neck, folding my fingers so my hands look like paws. I tense my shoulders then roll them back. Lick my teeth. Toby tenses his muscles, forcing me closer to the wall.

"Don't touch me, faggot."

"You're untouchable," he says, his eyes closed, motionless. Then a laugh escapes from him, like a bubble in a swimming pool.

We laugh for hours and hours.

There's a hand in my hair, stretching along my scalp. I was just falling asleep and now the sun is coming through the windows, flooding the room. "Get up," Yolanda says quietly.

"What are you doing here?"

She puts a finger to her lips, glances at Cateyes, who hasn't moved, the radio still playing beneath his head. I try to rub my eyes. I'm so tired. The clock reads 8 a.m. I can still feel the acid coursing through me. I feel like my skin is too tight over my bones and like my blood is thin and moving too fast.

"Yes," Yolanda says. "Get up. I'm not coming in early again."

We drive down 55th to the school. Yolanda drives a small Honda with a vanilla Christmas tree hanging from the mirror. I want to go back to sleep but more than that I want to stay in this car.

"We have a deal," she says in front of the school. She's turned the car off. We still have our seatbelts on. A line of kids are waiting to go in the main door. I don't recognize any of them.

"What deal?"

"You have to go to school for the rest of the week."

"Why would I do that?" Already I know I will, because I love her and she came to get me. The line is disappearing into the building. I'll do whatever she wants.

"Don't play games with me," she says. She's wearing short red shoes that match her lipstick. "I can't wake you up and drive you every day. You have to take responsibility for yourself. You know what I do when I'm not at Stevenson?" I shake my head. "I have a second job, in a club downtown, serving drinks to people that pay too much money for their clothes and don't know the value of anything. I have to pay all my student loans so I work eighty hours a week. I am not impressed by victims or by young men who don't take responsibility for themselves."

The line is gone. The stairs are cement and empty. The first bell has rung. The school looks like a fortress. "Can you take care of yourself?" she asks. "Or did I waste my time this morning?"

"I will."

"If you have perfect attendance for a week maybe I'll drive you again next Thursday."

"I can do that."

"I know you can. You can do anything you set your mind to."

"I've heard that one," I say, opening the car door.

"Be good," she calls after me.

Everyone is gathered at my doorway. Toby and Cateyes are having a face-off. Cateyes has been stealing from people. Toby went in Cateyes's drawers and found his sweater. Toby always wears Bugle Boy. We get $30 a month for clothing allowance. I bought a Bugle Boy shirt once to look like Toby and wore it when I went back to my old neighborhood. My friend Taro asked me why I was dressed like I was. "Are you hoping to grow into those clothes later?" he said. I haven't been back to my neighborhood since then. It's too far away anyway.

"Who said you could go through my drawers?" Cateyes asks. He peels his shirt off. We're like savages. Everybody is always half naked around here. He drapes his shirt over his dresser. He pushes his hands together, flexing his chest. I'm sitting on the end of my bed. The room smells of Cateyes's Aqua Velva, smells like he's been dumping it on the floor. This is not going to go well for me. Cateyes's body is compact, with muscle wrapping around him like rope. He gave himself the name Cateyes because he considers himself very good-looking. Once, he took off his glasses and told me to look into his eyes. "You see," he said. "Green, with gold flakes." But his eyesight keeps getting worse and his glasses thicker. His real name is Harmon. He's not who he thinks he is. He sits at night with workbooks studying for the GED, but he never learned how to read. Soon he'll be blind and I'll have to lead him around by the hand. He takes his glasses off and places them on top of his shirt. Toby and Cateyes are inches apart and Cateyes cranes his head. "You're next," he says to me over his shoulder. His body is the color of fake wood. Up and down his arms above his brand and around his chest are blue-ink tattoos too faded to be made out. The muscles in his back are like wings.

Hunter, John, Nettles, Waukee, Keef, and Dante are crowded behind Toby, stopping him from going somewhere. Everybody loves to see a fight. "Go, man," Dante says. Even I could beat Dante up. I hate him more than I hate anybody. He goes to all of his classes and collects his education bonus every week, which he keeps in a bank account. On Sundays his mother picks him up and takes him to church. She dresses fancy and always asks loudly if anyone would like to go with. We never say no, we just don't answer her. I like to think if my mother was still around and she came to see me here she'd bring something for everyone. People would be jealous because my mom is so cool. I want to do something horrible to Dante.

"You're a thief," Toby says, and Cateyes turns in one motion, his arm snaps, his fist landing in Toby's mouth. A loud crack, like a tooth breaking. Then Toby is swinging back in windmills. His arms are longer than Cateyes's but Cateyes is stronger. Toby is skinny. He's leaning back to create distance, but the crowd is forcing them together. I turn to the window. Kevin is outside, alone, shooting baskets and chasing down the ball. I can hear the ball bouncing above the screams. Kevin seems happy and oblivious. I wonder if Kevin's lonely. I would like to be lonely.

The fight tumbles back toward me and I jump out of its way onto my bed. Cateyes hits his head on my bed frame as they roll over each other. I can see everybody's head from where I'm standing and Cateyes's elbow, rising and falling, like a drill. The loud slaps of muscle and bone and the quiet scuffling against the furniture.

"What's going on up here?" It's Yolanda's voice, coming from the hallway. Cateyes's fist is raised, a thin smear of blood over his knuckles. Yolanda's arms at her sides, her long skirt with only her ankles showing before her flat shoes. She's so small, her body fills the door frame like a painting. I'm standing on my bed against the wall. The circle of boys tries to spread out but there's little room. Dante is the first to slide past Yolanda into the hallway. Cateyes stands; Toby doesn't get up.

"We're just playing," Cateyes says. Everyone is looking away somewhere, places just in front of their faces, empty spots.

"Playing is for children," Yolanda says. Nobody says anything. We've never seen her angry before. There's not enough of her to go around. It would take years to know somebody, meeting that person for one hour a week, and we don't have years. Her anger is gathering and I'm worried about what's going to happen. The worst thing you can call a child is a child. Someone should have told her that. I want to open the window and yell to Kevin to get upstairs quickly. I want to hide behind Yolanda and go with her when she leaves.

"Is this how you prove your manhood?" Yolanda asks. Cateyes's shoulders sink lightly. Waukee and Nettles squeeze past Yolanda and down the stairs. Keef and John follow. Cateyes moves to the dresser where he takes his glasses and wipes them with his shirt before putting them on. Hunter's looking at Yolanda, his thick hungry lips, chewing slowly as if he had grass in his mouth.

"You want to see my manhood?" Cateyes asks, unbuttoning his pants, showing his pubic hair. Yolanda's mouth opens, her clean red lipstick, her skin so creamy it's wet.

"C'mere," Hunter says suddenly, snatching at her sleeve. Yolanda yanks her arm up, backing out the doorway, her shirt catching on the latch. She pulls frantically and her sleeve rips. Hunter catches her wrist and shoves his fat hand inside her skirt, banging her into the open door, and Yolanda screams. Kevin looks toward my room and drops the basketball and runs inside. Hunter lets Yolanda go and she runs down the stairs.

The police have come and gone but they didn't take Cateyes away. Yolanda is gone and Veronica has taken her place. Veronica is the other female staff. She has a hole in her cheek the size of a filter and she swears at you if you ask her for anything but at least you know where you stand. Nobody likes Veronica. There'll be meetings tomorrow, social workers from downtown and the school. We'll lose privileges: phone, television, visitors. Toby is downstairs on the couch in the living room with ice on his face. I remember the knife beneath Toby's mattress and then Cateyes walks into the room. We have the largest bedroom and when I first came here people said I was lucky.

"Why do you let people go through my things?" Cateyes asks. Hunter's large shadow passes in front of the door and then disappears. I'm wondering if I tackle Cateyes whether I can hold him and make enough noise to avoid getting caught. I'm three inches taller than he is. But he would get me later. He'll get me when I'm sleeping, the way my father did once when he slipped on the ice on the stairs. I woke into my father's fists and then he dragged me by my hair to the steps to chisel away at the ice with a screwdriver. I can't be safe here. It's not enough to fight back one time. You have to fight back all the time. Fights never end until someone cuts you mouth to ear or your caseworker shows up and takes you to another home. But I'm the only one who thinks that way. My bed and Cateyes's are only three feet apart. Everybody else fights all the time. I'm the only one who's afraid.

Hunter's dark shape passes across the doorway again. I think of the shark coming up beneath the swimmer. "Why do you let people go through my things?" Cateyes repeats, as if someone had pressed rewind on a tape player. I turn my ear toward him. He squeezes his hands shut and looks back to the door but Hunter is gone. I squint my eyes closed for a second. This is not about me. This is about Hunter. Last night Hunter put his finger against Cateyes's temple as if his finger was a gun. "Beg for your life," Hunter said. "Say goodbye to your wife and children." It was a line from a movie. "Do him," Nettles said. "He wasn't never no Vice Lord." I almost sigh with relief. But it's too early. And I'm shaking. I can't help it. I've always been a coward. I feel my voice become a whisper.

"I wasn't," I say. "I wasn't here."

"Yo, Cat, let's get some Harold's," Hunter calls. Cateyes pushes my forehead with his palm. I try not to move. I keep my hands flat on my legs. Cateyes looks to me and the door. He makes a fist and puts his fist against my nose then kicks my laundry basket and my clothes fall onto the floor. He walks away.

In the living room Toby won't talk to me. I sit quietly, trapped. It's like I'm diseased. I want to be somewhere else. The staff office is off the entryway. Veronica is in there with the phone caught between her ear and shoulder and manila envelopes in her hand, the staff logs open in front of her. I see her through the Plexiglas wearing blue jeans and a brown belt. My first day here she received me and I sat in the office and she said I would like it here. She's hardly said anything to me since then. I get up and knock on the office door. She doesn't answer so I sit back down.

I sit quiet for a long time. In two years I'll be an adult. The living room is a couch with two chairs and a television. I don't want to feel sorry for myself but sometimes I do. The carpet is a strange green that doesn't resemble anything. I don't know where to go. The door is open; this is not a locked facility. I could walk through the Taylor Homes but all of the streets dead-end. They built them that way, dead ends and traps to prevent drive-bys. On the other side of the Taylors runs the Dan Ryan freeway and a fifty-foot drop into oncoming traffic. It's easy to get lost in there and each building is controlled by a different gang. Kevin's off work, in the Taylors somewhere. Those buildings are twenty-five stories high. In class the history book mentions them. I was surprised to see the buildings in our history book. The picture could have been taken from my window. They're the largest housing projects in the world and thirty thousand people live in them.

After a while John comes to me and punches my shoulder. I grip the sides of the chair, a scream caught in my throat. I put my hand over my face. Oh God, I think. "Hey man," he says. "There's nothing wrong with being scared."

* * *

Toby's lip is still swollen. He looks like a duck. But the fight is long over. Two days ago John and Nettles fought because John had said something that embarrassed Nettles at school. The fight ended with John holding Nettles in a bear hug, Nettles thrashing around, everything in John's room destroyed. Staff didn't come upstairs that time. Staff hasn't come upstairs since.

I look older than everyone here because I've grown a beard. Everybody pitched in and I bought bottles of Night Train and Mad Dog 20/20 at the liquor store near the metro. It's nearly dawn. We're shooting dice in Nettles' room. Dante is asleep in his bed. We're betting everything we have.

"Hold still," Cateyes says to me. I'm on the stool and he's giving me my first tattoo, a dagger on my left shoulder blade. He sterilized the pin by holding it over a lighter. He dips the pin into a bottle of India ink, one dot at a time.

Waukee lays fifty cents on the line and Nettles matches it, separating the two stacks with a pencil. Toby gives everyone cigarettes, even me, though we haven't spoken since he got beat up. "Bet," Nettles says. Waukee rolls a six.

The tattoo hurts but soon turns from pricks to a dull throbbing. Cateyes works slowly and carefully, pulling down on my skin with his other hand as if he were an artist. But he isn't, and his eyesight is bad. The tattoo is taking a bad shape. People keep handing me bottles, saying it will help with the pain. The girls came over yesterday. There was a new Hispanic girl, Maria, just admitted. She wore only pink, even pink earrings. Toby tried to talk to her but she wouldn't answer him. He offered her his watch but she shook her head. Cateyes sat on the front steps with Shoshanna. The rest of the girls stood near the fence smoking and we played basketball for them. "I'm in," Toby says, throwing a quarter on the floor.

"Too late, duck face," Waukee says.

Hunter says something unintelligible and laughs to him-self. He's holding a bottle against his large belly, and a long strand of snot is hanging from his nose. Everybody is ashing on the floor.

"How do you like that?" Cateyes asks. The dagger is off the hilt, and there's stray dots everywhere like blue freckles across my arm. He keeps pushing a towel against my arm and pulling it away. The pinholes are weeping blue ink and blood. It's a large tattoo; it covers my whole shoulder blade.

"It's great," I say. I feel dizzy.

"You ain't gonna believe it in the morning," Cateyes says.

"Is this just a dream?" I ask, joking.

"Shit," Waukee says. "Drink this and you'll fall over." He seems to be stumbling himself. The Mad Dog tastes like Orange Crush.

"I want to bet," I say.

"What do you got?" Nettles asks.

"I've got a necklace," I say. My mother's cheap chain with a phony silver dollar on it. They kept it for three years in a yellow pouch then handed it to me when they let me out. I'm ready to lose it.

"What do you want for it?"

"I got a quarter on Theo," John says.

"I'll take that bet," Toby says.

"I want your DCFS shirt," I say. Nettles has a long purple T-shirt with the number ten on the back. On the front it says Department of Children and Family Services. He never wears it outside of the house because he doesn't want people to know he's in a group home. I want the whole world to know.

"Get your necklace," Nettles says.

* * *

The necklace and shirt are next to each other on the carpet. My arm is throbbing and the room is starting to spin. "You should tattoo my face," I say. I shake the dice in both hands and blow on them. I throw the dice into the wall and they roll near Hunter's feet. If I lose this bet I'm wondering if I have anything else. I really want that shirt.

Six-four, a ten. "That's a tough throw," John says. "Unlucky. Pairs is different." Suddenly Dante lets out an enormous snore, like truck brakes. Everybody laughs and John drops his cigarette and it rolls underneath the bed where Dante is sleeping. We watch the cigarette. Dante's thin arm emerges from the blanket and scratches sleepily at the window. I throw the dice. They smack the wall and come up eight.

The cigarette is smoldering, darkening the carpet around its tip. Thick black smoke is rising from the bed frame. Dante lets out another snore, then a small sound like a cat crying. Nobody knows why he's here. His mom wears nice clothes and makeup. I feel for a second like I'm going to throw up, and then my stomach settles. I roll the dice again. Snake-eyes.

"C'mon Theo," John says. As if dice were a game of skill and I wasn't trying hard enough.

"Hey now," I say, turning the dice over in my palm, squeezing their edges. I have big hands. I should have been taller.

A small fire starts, like the wick of a candle. I think the fire is going to reach the mattress but nobody moves to do anything about it. We watch the flame jump. Will it go out?

"Dante," I say. "Starring in *The Burning Bed.*"

"Oh shit," John says, letting out a short breathy laugh. "That's my boy."

"Roll the dice, Theo," Nettles says. "Keep hesitating we're going to send you over to Price Home in a skirt." I think he wants to lose the shirt. I think he'll give it to me anyway because in another week he'll be in rehab and none of us will ever see him again.

"What do you have to do to set off a smoke alarm in this place?"

"Watch Dante light up the screen," John says. This time everybody laughs.

"Yeah, yeah. Absolutely," I say, shaking my hands over my head. I can feel my heartbeat in the dull throbbing pain in my arm. The fire spreads beneath the bed, a short half-inch flame the length of a sheet of paper. The bed sheet catches for a second, then the lit piece drops like water and goes out but the fire on the floor keeps burning. "He's famous. He's big time."

"His hottest role ever," John says. "His career is on fire. A trailblazing young actor." Hunter's laughing and his face is covered in snot and sweat. He looks like he was just born. Toby shakes his head and tries to take a drink from the Night Train but can't stop laughing and the wine pours from the sides of his mouth like blood. Dante turns over, rolling toward the wall, pulling his arms under his body, his butt appearing beneath the blanket.

"A star is born," I say, and throw the dice up in the air. The dice bounce on the carpet, tumbling against the dresser. A six. The ink has dribbled to my elbow. One of us should put the fire out. If we were somewhere else we probably would. But we're not somewhere else. This is where we live.

Nobody thought Yolanda would come back and she didn't. I never saw my caseworker either after he dropped me off here. Staff come and go all the time. I can imagine the conversation Yolanda had with her boyfriend. They were naked in bed, her small breasts, large red nipples. Everything about her was perfect. She said, *"Those children are monsters. You can't help them. We should put them in workfarms or in the desert."* And her boyfriend curled toward her, to smell her hair and her neck and to feel between her legs where it was warm and wet. He was glad because he didn't want to share her. *"They're only children. You just had a bad experience. Children need second chances." "Not these children,"* she said. *"There aren't enough chances in all the world for these children."* And maybe then they showered and had dinner and moved on to other topics. People that don't know any better are always optimistic. I see it on the news.

"You want that shirt or not?" Nettles asks. "You got some hoochie you're thinking about? You thinking about that Spanish girl that came in the van?" I pick the dice up as the flame is reaching the edge of the wall, blackening the corners.

"C'mon Theo, roll the dice."

"I want that shirt," I say, placing the dice on the floor in front of me, calculating the distance to the wall, lining them up, six-four, then taking them in my hand, careful to keep my head below the smoke.

"Win it then. Show us what you got."

CHAPTER NINE

STOP FIRST

THE HOSPITAL IS a long white room with two iron doors. The floor is white hexagonal tiles and there's steel webbing stretched so tightly over the windows it looks like it will snap. The hospital is attached to the juvenile detention center through a series of locked doors and elevators. They brought me here after Mr. Gracie stopped coming to work, leaving me unprotected, and Larry broke my leg. "Where's your boyfriend now?" Larry asked, while two other boys held me between the sinks by my throat and elbows. Larry kicked at my knee until there was a pop and all three of them ran out. My leg healed but I've been kept on the hospital ward instead of the detention center. Staff didn't want me to break my leg again. I stopped speaking for a month but nobody seemed to notice.

Time passes slowly without school classes or fights or games. Sometimes I play checkers with whoever's in the bed next to mine. Sometimes we play gin rummy. The lights swing on green chains from ceiling beams inside broken plaster. The kid on the end is cuffed to his bed and talks loudly about how dangerous he is and during lunch people throw butter packets at him. The doctors and nurses are friendly but cautious. The television only gets one channel which is filled with fuzzy soap operas during the day and Iran and Iraq at night. And things are usually quiet, and safe. Today I'm getting out.

"Ready?" my caseworker asks. He's the third caseworker I've had since I was eleven. There might have been a fourth who I never met. Adults come and go.

"Been ready," I tell him and he snorts. Everybody else looks away or pretends to be asleep. Most kids are only here for a few days except for me and Ricky, who's on dialysis. A doctor stands three beds down with a clipboard. I hold my arms out and my caseworker squeezes his handcuffs shut on my wrists, testing the chain with his index finger, pulling me forward as I stand up. I close my eyes and breathe for a second. It's better to be hand-cuffed in here anyway because when you're handcuffed it's like you don't have a face.

He leads me through the first set of doors, where the nurse is counting meds and stacking them next to a pile of Dixie cups and a plastic pitcher full of Kool-Aid. "Don't forget to visit," she says without looking up. Then a second door with a buzzer and a keylock. My caseworker leaves his key in the door and says, "Discharge, one custody," twice into a speakerphone. We stop in the bucket room for my belongings—a pair of jeans and my mother's necklace. The walls are grey steel boxes with numbers written over the front of them. The guard there and my caseworker exchange small talk. "Who you voting for?" "I'm voting for a forty hour week and a pay raise." "Heard that." We pass the secretary, a different secretary than the one that was here when I came in, down to the courtroom area where a line of parents and children are waiting to be searched by an officer at the end of a conveyer belt. We pass under a sign that says

DCFS ID Badge Required No Re-Entry.

Outside it's hot and wet. It's the middle of summer and the sky is white. My caseworker slips a hand under my armpit as we cross to a new three-story parking lot. I wonder what else has changed in the time I've been inside. A large black woman passes us with her hand around the back of a child's neck and stares briefly at my handcuffs and clucks her tongue and smiles as if I'd done something cute.

We stop at a tan Toyota with rust around the wheel-wells. There's a puddle of bright green liquid in front of the car. I lean against the mirror while he squats near the bumper and sticks his finger in the puddle. He looks disappointed and shakes his hand, wiping his finger on the hood.

"Japs ripped me off," he says. "I just got this car. Used." He turns the ignition and the car starts and I grab the seatbelt awkwardly with both hands and pull it across my lap. "Do you know anything about cars?" he asks.

"I'm only fourteen," I tell him.

"I thought you were fifteen."

"Next week."

"Happy birthday then." He opens the glove compartment, sees nothing in it, and slams it shut before throwing the car into gear. "Probably a pin leak. I'll pour some glue in there. That stuff fixes everything." He shows his ID to a man inside a glass box at the bottom of the ramp and the man waves him past. The red radiator light and the yellow engine light are lit on the dashboard. "There's some bad news," he says, guiding the car into traffic, stopping at a light behind a chicken truck.

The last time he came was the first time I met him. He sat on the edge of my bed and told me a Christian family was going to adopt me. He was hyper and spoke fast, checking his watch between sentences and shaking his leg. I thought he was on drugs. He said they were very Christian, had three daughters and a swimming pool. "You ever prayed before?" he asked. He said the foster family lived near Harlem Irving Plaza.

But we're not going in that direction. I'm still wearing hand-cuffs and we're heading south on Lake Shore Drive between the water and downtown. Grant Park is littered with tents, looks like a festival. He shakes a cigarette out of a pack in his breast pocket.

"The mother's sick," he says. "Real sick. When you're sick the church absolves you from your Christian responsibilities." He punches a button on the dashboard and warm air blows in from the vents. "That was a joke, lighten up. We couldn't leave you in Western anymore. There was a court order." He looks at me and takes his cigarette out of his mouth, makes a point in the air with it. The car is a mess and I pick up a ticket stub for *The Empire Strikes Back,* then drop it back to my feet. His lips are almost orange; his bangs are wet and stuck to his forehead. He looks like he's dying. People are bicycling on the path next to the lake and the lake is filled with sailboats and somewhere in the distance a metal structure sits on the water. I was a year late getting out. I shouldn't have still been there when Larry decided to break my leg.

"You know what?" he says. I don't answer. We pass Soldier Field, then the McCormick Center. "I have fifty other kids like you I'm responsible for. You all think you're special. You should try paying rent, see what that's like. You get a roof over your head, three meals a day. Try working for DCFS—you don't know the meaning of the word *underfunded.* Working for DCFS is like trying to convince someone to sell you a shirt for a dime. So don't look at me like that. Where you're going, we've decided, is a good place."

"Who decided?"

"The judge."

I think I'm hungry but I'm not sure. I'm hungry and nauseous. I wonder what that judge looked like. I've been at court four times but only once taken inside the courtroom. I was in court number six, which is one they use for custody hearings involving the state. If the hearing is between parents it happens in courtrooms nine through twelve. We're not supposed to be allowed in court but they brought me in.

The lawyer for the state looked like a lumberjack. He wore a red shirt and a beige jacket, and he said my name while pulling a manila envelope out of a suitcase. I was standing only one person away from him but he didn't even look at me. He'd probably been carrying me in his suitcase for weeks. As far as he and the rest of them were concerned I was that envelope. He handed it to my guardian *ad litem,* who opened it and looked inside like he'd dropped a quarter, then turned it over to the judge. The judge opened it and started to read the pages, moving her lips but not saying anything, occasionally underlining something. Everybody stayed quiet while she read; nobody looked at each other. There weren't that many pages, maybe ten. At one point she looked confused and rubbed two fingers across her eyebrows.

"What's it say?" I asked.

"Who the fuck let him in here?" the DCFS lawyer said. The judge peered up from the papers, fixing me for a second over her glasses, then returned to her reading. My guardian put his hand on my shoulder and an officer escorted me out of the courtroom and sat me on a bench.

"Sit here," the officer said, then walked away.

I've heard of other kids being brought into the court. I heard of one kid who was left in one of the courtrooms after the building had closed and they found him there in the morning, sleeping in the bailiff box, and brought him upstairs to the detention center.

I sat there for half an hour and I guess I thought I was going to get out that day. I thought that's why I had been in the court-room, but when my guardian came to get me he told me not to worry, then walked me back up the stairs to the detention cen-ter. I shouldn't have been surprised. That night Mr. Gracie slid his key into my door. Petey stayed sleeping, his large back fac-ing the room. In the last office on the floor, under a single unpro-tected lightbulb, I took my clothes off and folded them into the corner. Mr. Gracie lifted my chin and asked me what was wrong. "You look like somebody stole your candy." I started to cry for the first time since the state took custody of me. Once I started I couldn't stop. I didn't know where it was coming from but I felt like I had failed everybody. He kept his hand over my face, barely covering my mouth and nose. "This is the place for that," he said. "Go ahead and cry here." When I finally stopped he waited a second, wiping my face with his palm. "Are you done?" I nodded and he slapped me hard. "Be quiet now." He gripped my hair and pulled me across the steel table until the table edge was against my thighs. "Don't move at all." The next day I could still feel his hand across my face. Soon after that he stopped com-ing to work.

At 55th Street we turn inland past the Museum of Science and Industry and the school buses in the parking lot. There's a sign with Jimmy Carter's face graffitied over with a six point star. "You have a girlfriend?" my caseworker asks. I wonder if he knows anything at all about what happens in a juvenile deten-tion center.

"I don't," I say.

"You gay?"

"No."

"I just broke up with my girlfriend," he says, taking the unlit cigarette out of his mouth. "Get this. She's been with her room-mate the whole time we've been together. I mean, it wasn't her roommate at all, it was her boyfriend, they were living together, trying to have children. Serious. She never wanted me to come over to her place but I insisted so finally she had me over for lunch. We're having soup and this guy just walks in and introduces himself as Sandra's boyfriend. We were having lunch in his house—I guess she didn't expect him to come home. He didn't know either. And you know what she says? She says 'I guess I screwed up.' She guesses she screwed up. We were both dating the same woman for nearly two years. Can you believe that? You think that kind of stuff only happens on television but it happens in real life too." He puts the cigarette back in his mouth and looks to me for a response.

"That sucks," I say.

"Sucks is right. You've never been lied to until you've been lied to by a woman. I should take you to see her, then you'd know what a bitch looks like. That could be some useful knowledge as you get older. Save you some heartache." He nods his head as if it was attached to his neck by a spring. "That's what I should do alright."

We pass Cottage Grove, then the north-south train tracks. The buildings deteriorate the further we get from the lake until the landscape is unrecognizable. The streets are rubble, old unlived-in three-flats missing walls and roofs, bricks in the gutters. This must be what it looks like after a war. At Washington Park he finally lights his cigarette. "Can I have one?" He looks at me with his cigarette bit between his teeth, then reaches into his shirt and hands me a cigarette and holds out his own so I bend to light mine from the tip of his. He smells like a tin can, and while I'm leaning toward him he turns and I bump my head against his shoulder. "Watch yourself," he says.

After the park the street signs disappear and the projects start and the giant building shadows cover the gravel lots and stores with no names on them except the names spray-painted on their side. "If they knew anything they'd level this fucking zoo."

People are everywhere, standing next to headless poles on the sidewalks, kneeling over dice and stacks of coins, crossing the street, ignoring the cars. Some people aren't wearing shoes; others are wearing bathrobes. Nobody seems to care. He's getting nervous. His orange lips turning pink. We pass an empty playground, a blur of paint splashed over iron and rubber, and enter a side street where the car dips hard in a pothole, the carriage banging over the asphalt, and I put both hands against the dashboard as the tremors pass through the frame. Then we stop at a driveway in front of a square red house with a front yard full of dirt. Three boys sit on the porch below a sign that reads STEVENSON HOUSE. My caseworker pulls the keys and they rattle in his hand. "Shit." He takes a deep breath. He's deciding whether to get out of the car with me or whether to just tell me to go and drive away. He can't wait to be rid of me so he can get back to his girlfriend and his own problems but I don't care. I know this is a bad place. I also know it's better than the place I left behind. I stretch my arms out to him and he leans away first before moving forward to unlock my wrists. He takes his handcuffs back, fastening them inside his jacket.

"Here," he says, offering me another cigarette. I take it from him and slide it behind my ear. I wait with him, the car heating up. "Tell them I had a meeting and I'm sorry I wasn't able to come inside." We sit for what feels like a long time without talking before I finally reach for the handle. I get out of the car, rubbing my wrists, and shut the door behind me. One of the boys picks up a small rock and throws it lazily in my direction. The stone bounces past my foot, pinging against a hubcap.

CHAPTER TEN

THE YARD

AT NIGHT, WHEN our door is locked, we aren't supposed to be talking. We're supposed to be sleeping. I stand over Petey, naked except for my underwear. The springs creak and I hold my breath before placing my hands on the sill. We can never tell if they can hear us or not. Through the window I make out the dark outline of the Henry Horner housing projects, the sharp corners facing Western, and some of the dull grey towers of the University campus and its cement bridges crossing between the building's top floors. I think about University sometimes but I would never go to a school near here. If I ever get out I'll go somewhere far away, another city on the edge of the country.

"See any birds?" Petey asks in a low whisper. He turned six-teen yesterday, three years older than me, but we don't celebrate birthdays here. "Anything?" Petey lies under his blanket, his legs inches from my feet. I think about stepping on his ankles for some height.

"I can see the Circle Campus. And the highway. Same stuff.

That's the Roosevelt entrance," I tell him, nodding toward something he can't see. "Goes straight to Wisconsin."

Petey shifts below me and I catch his sour odor escaping from under his blanket. "Be careful," Petey says. Things have been tense recently, more than usual. There have been rumors. Not that anyone talks to us. But you can't help but hear in the school, or in food line, people whispering threats to one another. We listen for footsteps, for a trustee or a guard to swing the door open and pull one of us out of the room. I think about the door opening all the time, even when I'm on the other side of it. Petey does too. That's why he wets his bed.

Petey stares at me with his huge misshapen head. I try to see further. I love the streets. I can name every fourth street in Chicago. I wasn't looking out of this window until recently, when we began to talk. Now I climb on his bed every night to look outside and when I'm looking outside I want to jump up and down on the bunk, but I don't.

Before, I didn't want to talk to Petey because of the way he looks and the way he smiles a lot. I knew the minute I saw him he was a victim. The first time he came into this room I folded my arms over my head and ducked between my knees. It was like a hole had opened in the floor. After that, if he would say something I would look away like I hadn't heard. I stayed close to the wall, on my side of the room. I spent months not communicating with him. And one day, not so long ago, they beat him up in the bathroom; they always get him there, but maybe this time was worse. I was under the last shower and still covered in soap. He was lying on the tiled floor wheezing, his teeth broken in pieces, the pink halo around his head sliding toward the drainpipe. I tried to look ahead and get the soap off my legs but I couldn't stop staring at him. And he said, "I wonder what they wanted." Then he tried to laugh but started to choke and had to stop. But he made it clear, he wasn't going to hold it against me. He didn't expect me to help.

Now we talk about cars, or about television. Or bands, not that there's ever any music in here. But mostly cars. We both like big cars a lot. I tell him my father drove a 1970 Cougar convertible with a white leather interior, the original hubcaps, and a 351 Quickstart engine. And everything is fine, except when Petey asks me personal questions like about Tuesday nights. "Don't ask about that," I tell him. But not too long ago I wouldn't have answered him at all.

I crawl under the sheet and the blue knit blanket. I always try to keep the sheet between my body and the blanket. They don't wash the blankets. We sleep in our underwear, our clothes in the hallway next to our shoes. I close my eyes and think of nice things to dream about. I think about driving in my father's convertible, sitting on his lap while he shows me how to drive around the lot at Warren State Park, the basketball courts in front of us, and the hill where I would sled in the winter. I try not to think about the burned-out shell of the car sitting in the alley, cinder and twisted carriage, waiting for my father's friend with the truck to come and tow it away.

"People and Folk," Marco whispers to me and Petey at breakfast. The breakfast hall is rows of brown tables, one after another, thirty tables in two columns. Three long Plexiglas windows with steel wire running through them. Open seating divides itself by basic distinctions, People or Folk, the two largest Chicago gangs, and within those, subgroups: Deuces, Black Gangster Disciples, Assyrian Eagles, Vice Lords, Gay Lords, Latin Kings, Simon City Royals. Five points and six points, pitchforks and crowns. A separate table for the unaffiliated Knights of Kaba, a Muslim gang from Hyde Park. And within those groups color lines, ethnicities, neighborhoods, age. Central Park and Wilson, Farwell and Clark, Sixty-third and Cottage Grove. The intersections of Chicago meet here in the boys' Juvenile Hall, the tables named after street corners. Toward the back of the room the boys get thinner and smaller and younger. Finally, outcasts, victims, fodder. Where we sit. There are two tables of us, the ugliest and the weakest, and we don't even like each other.

Petey smiles and shakes his head, which I take to mean he doesn't understand. Petey doesn't understand anything. He's just big and dumb and ugly. But I understand what Marco is saying. Marco has short blond stubble and nods rapidly as he eats. Things are coming to a head. There's a new inmate somewhere and it's someone from the upper ranks. The soldiers are going to be expected to perform. It's going to go off, and that's why there's the tension and the quiet. The two largest organizations. The worst possible news. Marco forces his entire strip of bacon into his mouth. I take a spoonful of oatmeal. Marco squints his mean eyes and looks at me as he chews.

Ms. Jolet has wide hips and long black hair. She runs basic math problems on the board and I copy them into my book. I like her, even when she's turned away, with chalk in her hand. She's always upbeat. "You have to start each day happy," she says. She wears bright lipstick, and her ears are full of jewelry. People are always trying to get her attention and she has a way of sharing it, which I hate. I watch her move and how the fabric of her dress hangs on her waist and then outlines her legs, where she is most fat, and fantasize about what she would do to me if she could keep me after school. *Come here, Theo. Closer.* I dream about being only six inches tall and Ms. Jolet taping me to the inside of her thighs, her giant legs crossing back and forth over me, and walking out of the building with me inside her skirt. Behind me the boys pass notes back and forth. Something hits the back of my head. I grab the wet paper with two fingers and let it drop to the floor. This is the good class, for kids that don't get in trouble, kids who don't need as much supervision. I copy the multiplication tables. I understand them now. I'm learning. I think I'm on track for my age, but I'd have to see the other tracks to know. Before noon I raise my hand and ask if I can use the bathroom. Ms. Jolet says yes.

The halls are marked with red dashes that run five feet off the wall. The floor is the color of bone. When we're in line we have to walk along the dashes, only turning when one group of dashes meets another group of dashes. When walking alone we have to stay between the dashes and the wall. I wear a necklace with a plastic hall pass. Because of my status I can go to the bathroom unescorted. I pass a boy walking in handcuffs flanked by two guards. They're talking about something that has nothing to do with the boy between them and one of the guards takes a long slow look at me as we pass.

I wash my hands before moving to the urinals. As I'm peeing Larry walks into the bathroom and steps to the urinal next to me. Larry is a Vice Lord, one of the heads, slated to join the El Rukns when he turns eighteen. He sits at the front table in the mess hall. Larry looks like he's made out of bowling balls but he's not much older than me. Maybe a year. His mouth is a thin line, like the cartoon Iron Man. "You're not very big there," Larry says looking down at my penis. I feel my cheeks go red and my breathing get heavy. My peeing slows down. "What's wrong?" Larry asks. "I make you scared?"

"No," I answer. When I first came into Western I had sat at the wrong table and Larry reached across the table and pulled my face into his plate of mashed potatoes and meatloaf. Larry held me there, my hands gripping the ends of the table but I couldn't pull away because it felt like I'd rip my hair out if I tried to move. "What are you doing at this table?" Larry asked, lifting my head up and ramming me down into the plate a few times, smearing the potatoes on my cheeks, the other boys laughing, their plates shivering on the wood, the guards ignoring the obvious. Finally he let go and I stood up, my legs weak, my face a mess of food and gravy. I slowly carried my plate to the back of the room and sat down, wiped the food from my face with a napkin, then stared straight ahead to the wall until the period was over. That was a year ago.

Larry beat me up a lot when I first came here. He came up to me on the school yard and hit me with both his fists, in my back and my front, my wind leaving me. "Look," he said to his friends. "He doesn't even fight back." Then one day Mr. Gracie asked me where I got the black eye from. I was seated naked on the desk in front of him and he held my chin in his hand. It was cold. I shook my head and Mr. Gracie let go of me then smacked me across the face and I said "No." I kept my arms at my sides. But then Mr. Gracie hit me again and I said it was Larry and Larry never touched me after that.

"You know what's going to happen tonight?" Larry asks, pulling his pants up, rolling them over his penis deliberately. "Gonna be a big fight. Whose side you on?"

"I'm not on anybody's side," I tell him and move with an affected calm to the sink and run the water, turning over my hands. I have long, thin scars on my left arm from my elbow to my wrist. Each time I look they seem more faded and farther away.

"In all that commotion I could probably stab you. Nobody would notice. That's messed up, right?"

I dry my hands on the towel, turn to walk out of the bathroom. Larry is there, in front of me, blocking the way. I try to go around him and he moves with me, so that I would have to bump him if I'm going to get by.

"Where you going?"

"Back to class."

"Back to class," Larry mimics. I feel my stomach snap closed and a wave of nausea pass through me. "That's messed up, right? That I might stab you." I look at my shoes, the yellow laces running through my sneakers. Larry hits me beneath my chin and my teeth clatter together. "You afraid of me?" I shake my head. "Why you looking away then? Something in your eye?" I look straight ahead into his face. Larry smiles at me. "I'm only playing with you. You know that. You gonna tell your bodyguard?"

"No."

"You gonna tell your boyfriend?"

Larry moves aside and I step into the halls, which are empty, and past the dorm rooms. I try to catch my breath but my neck is tightening on me. I stick my tongue out of my mouth, stretch my lips as far as they will go. I pull on the corners of my mouth with my fingers. The floor shifts. I turn the corner toward class and stop and place my hands on my thighs. I let the fear run out of me, drain from my nose and my eyeballs. Wait for my breath to come back.

They don't give us knives. It's hamburger night. Hamburger and French fries, so even the fork is unnecessary, but there it is. "You gonna eat that?" Marco asks and I shake my head. Marco pushes the hamburger into his face, filling his white spotty cheeks with the meat patty and the dry bread.

"You know what we should do," Petey says. "We'll start our own basketball team. If we practice every day we can probably play for the Chicago Bulls. It's just practice. Why not?"

Marco snorts but the food in his mouth stops him from saying anything.

"You can play basketball, right?" Petey says to me. There's basketball in the yard after dinner but Petey and I never get to play. We hang out with Marco by the back, hoping not to be noticed.

"I'm too short," I tell him.

"You'll grow. I bet you're seven feet before you're twenty. How tall are you now?"

"Five six."

"Seven feet for sure."

"How tall are you, Marco?"

"Fuck you, Petey."

I turn away. Sometimes the optimism in Petey's voice is disturbing. I turn back to my fork and its dull points. Not much of a weapon. I wouldn't use it anyway. And I don't have pockets, nowhere to put it. And it would probably be noticed, and that would be worse. Mr. Gracie can protect me from the other kids but not from the other guards. The guards can do anything. They make you hold out your hand and they hit you as hard as they can on your palm with a spoon. The pain rumbles through your whole body. They restrained one kid by tying him to a table. Then they forgot about him. They left him in a room tied to a table for three days, then he was taken to the hospital ward and treated for dehydration. Another guard choked a kid to death. Everybody knows about it. Nobody says anything. That guard stands at the front of the room by the food line, a big man with a sloping forehead and an enormous hard round gut hanging over his belt. There were talks of investigations but nothing came of it.

Things seem normal enough. Still air and the sound of chewing. The meat smell. It's not going to happen here. It's not going to happen during dinner. I turn to Marco, who, done with his food, also looks around nervously. We're unaffiliated. Traffic will not stop for us.

"It's going to happen in the yard," Marco says.

"I know. I know." I touch the fork prongs. Hold the fork with one hand and gently push my other hand onto it.

"If you were seven feet tall," Petey says, "you'd get every rebound."

"If I was seven feet tall I'd put on a cape and fly away."

"We need a plan." Marco wipes his mouth with the napkin. Of the three of us Marco is the only one who is actually a fighter. He's held his own in most fights so far but he knows he is marked because of the swastika tattoo on his left forearm. Marco came into Western a month ago. He told me it was for setting fire to a synagogue but I doubted it. I haven't told Marco that I'm half Jewish. It isn't the kind of thing that's worth telling anybody in here. Marco got an early reputation for biting people during fights in the bathroom, trying to gouge eyes out with his thumb. "So what is it?" he asks.

"What's the plan?" I say.

"What are we going to do?" Marco says, shaking his head. The fork is about to break the skin on my palm and I hold it for a moment to feel the pain. The sound and the smell goes away. The room is a TV set on mute. I pull my hand off and the pain stops and the sound comes back. In front of us hundreds of other boys eat. Some with shaved heads, the newer boys still with the hair they came in with, all of the heads bobbing over the sea of plates. The guards standing along the walls like sleeping bulls. Fluorescent bulbs swinging on chains above us. All of us in for different reasons. All of us waiting to go to the yard.

* * *

At 6:30 two hundred boys line up outside the TV room in a single file. A guard takes attendance, occasionally pulling someone out of the lineup to be escorted somewhere. We stand in order of age, with the youngest, the twelve-year-olds, at the very back, even though one of the twelve-year-olds, Anthony, threw another child off the roof of a building and is being tried as an adult.

We march with six guards. We wear our assigned clothes, brown pants with elastic waistbands that read PROPERTY OF DOC on the front as if someone was going to try to steal them, or us. T-shirts color-coded by group, green for owls, blue for bears. Nobody seems sure what the animal designations are supposed to mean. Everything is a system but none of it works. I was ordered released three months ago by a judge on the first floor of this very building but nothing came of it. I wasn't even handcuffed. I didn't even know I had a court date. I was pulled out of the line before breakfast. They walked me out the heavy, main door, past the office workers, down two flights of stairs, through the metal detectors and the windows and the security gates to the court rooms. They told me to sit down on a bench and they left me alone for an hour while I watched parents bring their children in and out of the room in front of me. Finally a man in a thin shirt with a small, sharp beard introduced himself as my guardian *ad litem*. I'd never seen him before. He was eating an orange, which he peeled with his thumbs, and he had a plastic Jewel Foods bag full of papers. He said I'd be heading to placement, maybe a specialized foster home. Would I like that? He seemed nervous. He wanted to know how they were treating me upstairs. Any problems? He put his hand covered in orange juice on my shoulder. I couldn't figure out who he worked for or what he was trying to tell me or what he wanted me to tell him. What if I said, "He takes me to the last room by the fire exit and I take my clothes off and bend over the table there. Sometimes I feel bad because

I never put up a fight. The other boys are waiting to kill me, but Mr. Gracie protects me." What if I said that? Probably Mr. Gracie would be gone and Larry and the other boys would cut me into tiny pieces and that would be the end of it. The judge ordered me fit for placement, which means I should be in a group home. Before leaving, my guardian said it was just a matter of processing some paperwork. They took me back upstairs and I waited. I waited on my mat, I waited in the lunchroom and the classroom and the TV room. I stopped sleeping. I almost told Mr. Gracie, who had told me never to say anything when we were together unless I was asked a question. I almost told Mr. Gracie one Tuesday night after Mr. Gracie had closed the door and pointed with his right hand toward the corner of the room, "I'm going to get out of here." But I didn't. I've never disobeyed Mr. Gracie and occasionally Mr. Gracie says, his hand over my face covering my mouth, pinching my nose shut, "You're a good kid. Well behaved. You're going to turn out OK."

We trickle, one at a time, through the double steel doors onto the yard. The stronger kids walk casually toward the lone basketball hoop, Larry dribbling the basketball. The rest of us just mill around. It's a cold, damp day. The sky is the same color as the walls. There's a tetherball stand where a leather bag hangs from a long rope. Usually there's a game of tag and there's card games, spades, hearts, and bid whiz. And usually the basketball game is so intense that others wait to play, watching the guys in the game lunging at the hoop, sweat soaking into the collars of their shirts. But today just a handful of boys throw the ball toward the basket, then let it bounce away on the cement. Nobody lays any cards out. No one goes near the tetherball. Other groups walk slowly into corners or lean against the walls.

Marco catches up with me. His face is red as a beet. "Did you see that?"

"See what?" Nobody has a jacket and usually when it's cold like this they'll take us to the gym or just leave us in the TV room.

"They know, you fucking jerk," Marco spits at me. Petey joins us as we walk toward our spot against the wall, near the back but not in the corners. The corners are taken.

"Hey," Petey says.

"The guards," Marco continues. "The guards know. Look at how they were acting. And where are they now? They're gone. They are gone. Oh man. Motherfuckers. *Motherfuckers*."

I turn around and see it's true, and that groups of boys are congealing together like oil cooling in a pan. Across the top I see Larry whispering in someone's ear then turning in my direction. A smile spills across Larry's face when he notices me looking at him. Larry lifts his shirt slightly and I see the flat slab of metal then the shirt lowering back over the blade like a curtain. My view is obstructed by bodies swelling the yard.

"I'm Jewish," I say to Marco, sticking my thumbs in the elastic of my pants. The sky spinning above us.

"What?"

"On my father's side," I tell him. "I'm half Jewish."

"Why would I give a shit about that?"

"You'd care on the outside," I tell him.

"We're not on the outside, are we peckerwood? Does this look outside to you?"

Groups are moving together, forcing toward the center of the yard. We try to push through but find ourselves stuck in the coming waves. I lean back and realize that Marco is there behind me and Petey's big shoulder is in my arm. We have formed a triangle. I look through the crowd for Larry's knife. There's a scream through my ear. He's been waiting to do it to me. He has. Waiting. He's been waiting since Mr. Gracie smacked him in the teeth with his club and pointed to me and told Larry, anything else happens to me Larry was going to take a long fall. The kind of fall you don't get up from. Mr. Gracie sealed my fate then. He must have known he couldn't always be there for me. Now I'm doomed. I wait for the blade in my stomach, peeling the skin from my ribs. For a second I close my eyes.

The sound of a jaw breaking echoes through the noise. Fists and faces. There are teeth biting near my nose and Petey's shoulder covering my face then jerking away. The boys rush together. The air burns. The arms swing in windmills. Blood flies against the blacktop. All over is smashing and punching. A fist hits my cheek, the ground flies toward me. The asphalt beneath my fingers is full of pebbles and I'm surrounded by knees bumping my ears. I am lifted by my collar from the crowding feet. I turn around and see Marco has gone down and is sitting in a position that resembles a prayer. But then Marco is standing again, his arms bent into his chest, feet planted, chin forward. The triangle between us grows larger. I stretch my arms in front of me, sucking air through my wide-open mouth. Guards are rushing into the yard, swinging billy clubs. A gunshot. They're herding us toward the walls. Voices come from the loudspeakers shouting unintelligible directions but repeating them over and over again until they make sense.

"Line up against the wall, single file. Line up against the wall, single file. Line up against the wall, single file."

We're against the wall, our backs facing out, our legs spread, our hands pressing into the stone. Petey is on the other side of me, his head down. A smile grows across my face. Marco turns his head slightly and we look at each other and I think Marco is going to start laughing. His face is contorting, his eyes squeezing shut involuntarily, and tears are running over his cheek, pooling into his mouth. He's mewing, his tongue licking at the puddles. Behind us, someone is dead. But it isn't us. A doctor is examining a boy who is lying in the middle of the yard with a pitchfork carved into his chest. It isn't us. We're fine.

I grab the bed rail and place my foot against the base and swing around it, wrapping my other leg around the pole. This is life. I spin three times this way before I sit down on the bed across from Petey. I'm dizzy and Petey deals me seven cards. I look at my cards and like them. "So how'd you get here?" I ask. I might be feeling more talkative than I've ever felt. I organize first by color and then by rank. The lights are on. Western is under lockdown. There won't be school tomorrow, and they'll feed us in our room. And maybe the day after that, but then Mr. Gracie will come for me, late at night.

"Stealing," Petey says as an answer, laying a card down, drawing from the deck. "Driving around. I would steal cars."

"Where would you go?"

"The suburbs."

What's done is done. It won't happen again for a while. I'll be gone before the next riot. I've got my walking papers. They can't hold me in here forever. They'll find a placement for me soon. I'll be transferred. Things will be okay and I'll start over, like I always do. When I get out I'm going to learn how to fight. I'm going to stop being scared. I'll change completely.

"And you?" Petey asks.

I sit back on his bunk, back against the wall, the window above my head. I grab Petey's foot. "Ha," I say, and shake his foot. I lay down three hearts, the king, the queen, and the jack. That's ten points each but there's still an ace that goes on the end and the ace is worth fifteen. I discard a low spade and Petey finishes my run on both sides, with the ace and the ten.

"Generous of you," he says. We'll never be this close again.

"I couldn't stay put," I tell him, picking one up. I measure my options. One of Petey's eyes is higher than the other. I should be able to win this. My grandfather was a card player. My father told me once that his dad had bet their house and lost. He used to tell me I looked like my grandfather. I try to answer Petey but I don't really know the answer. I pull on my nose. "I was in CYS, emergency placement. There were thirty of us in each room and there were four rooms. There was only two staff members and they stayed in the office with the door locked. I tried to ask them when I was getting out but they wouldn't tell me. Then one of the ladies opened the door and said to me, If you don't like it here, why don't you walk away? It's not like you're in jail. She had hair on her chin. She was the bearded lady. And it was true, the door was open. So I did it. I just left. And she yelled after me where was I going. I said I was going home. I went back to my old neighborhood, but everyone was gone. And when they caught me they put me here."

CHAPTER ELEVEN

HOME BEFORE THE LIGHTS

I TAG THE base and stop, grip my legs, take a deep breath, and shake the sweat from my forehead. "I'm too fast," I tell Sammy, who didn't catch the ball on time and slaps my side with it anyway. "Safe," I tell him, nearly falling off the base.

"You think so?" He tosses the ball back to his brother Edward. Fifth grade is going to end in a week. The breeze is blowing hard, it could rain soon.

"Could you imagine being as fast as me?" I ask.

"Must be great," he says.

"It's the greatest thing in the world," I tell him.

Taro is on the other base singing, "That's the way, uh huh uh huh, I like it." Four is a good number for a game of running bases, but five is even better, harder to get stuck between the two throwers. With five players you can place the bases further apart. Sometimes Justin plays, but his dad wouldn't let him out today.

"You're out," Edward says.

"Shit," Taro says. Taro stepped off the base. Taro likes to swear. Two years ago, in third grade, I met Taro in the bathroom and he said, "Motherfucker." He spit in the urinal and put his hand inside his pants and waited to see what I would do. "That's nothing," I told him. "My father says worse things than that all the time. My dad's a cuss faucet." Then Taro wrote *Mr. Petak is a jingle balls* on the wall in black marker. He handed me the marker and I drew a balloon with a smiley face on it and wrote *Don't Pop Me* beneath it. "That's retarded," he said. We've been best friends ever since.

Taro and Edward switch places and Taro bounces the ball impatiently. Taro's got a bad temper. Now Edward and I are runners. Edward is bigger than the rest of us, but he's kind of girly. He's fat, but not in front like Gus Strylopalus. Edward's fat hangs around his waist. Sometimes at school people call him sissy. His sisters are fat too, but they don't look so bad. For bases we use Sammy and Edward's jackets. We play in the middle of the alley in front of the garage. Sammy and Edward live in the only house on the block, a blue and white house with a big green backyard. Everybody else lives in apartments. I live in the corner building with my father, my mother, and sometimes my father's girlfriend who comes over and stays for days at a time. He doesn't think I know she's his girlfriend. He says she's there to take care of my mother. My mother is not well. He says Claire is my mother's best friend, but I don't think she is.

I'm sprinting under the net and stop at the base. Taro misses the ball that Sammy has launched to him. He had to throw the ball over me; you're not allowed to hit the runner. The ball bounces down the alley and Taro takes off after it. A dog starts barking. Sammy and I cross each other, then run back again, then again. We do the dance that you do when you steal three bases in a row.

Taro is all the way down at the end of the alley and walking back with the ball in his hand. He's red-faced. "Why don't you

learn how to throw?" Edward asks Sammy. Sammy is only nine.
He's lucky we play with him.

"I can throw," Sammy says.

"You throw like a pigeon swims," Edward says.

"What?"

"Fuck you guys," Taro says, standing on the base next to
Edward. He bounces the ball.

"Shut up," Sammy says. "My dad will hear you."

"Fuck your dad," Taro says. "Fuck your dad twice, with a
metal broomstick, in the ass."

"What did you say?" Edward says, turning around.

"Don't let your ass get your mouth in trouble," Taro says.
He's been saying that for six months. He looks at me and jerks
his thumb toward Edward, rolling his eyes like Edward is crazy.
Suddenly Taro turns, screaming, his tongue out of his mouth, his
eyes crossed. "Wazzow!" Taro yells. Edward jumps. Taro tags
him. "You're it. Ha ha, fatso."

Edward takes the ball and throws it to his brother. Then he
tramps under the basketball net, opens the gate to his yard, and
walks inside his house without looking back. "Where are you
going?" Taro asks. "I thought we were friends forever." He's
answered by the sound of the back door, which sounds like a can
dropping.

Sammy looks at the ball in his hand, then Taro, then me.
I shrug my shoulders. Sammy runs into the house after Edward.

"Now what do you want to do?" Taro asks, leaning against the
garbage can. He hands me his cigarette and I take a drag, then
hand it back to him. He doesn't know that I've been practicing.
I bought a pack of cigarettes from the Marlboro machine at
Poppin' Fresh and I've been sneaking out at night and smoking

them down the block. Smoking makes me dizzy, but I'm getting better at it. At first I didn't inhale.

"I don't know," I say. "I don't care. Just hang out."

"I can't wait until I'm older," Taro says. "Then I can have a car and a gun. I'm going to join the army and kill gooks." I shake my head. On the television all week, the helicopters have been taking the last Americans out of Vietnam. Taro is Chinese.

"What if someone shoots you by mistake?" I ask.

"Watch it," he says. "You're on dangerous ground."

My dad says that the Vietnamese cheated us. He says they shot down our pilots and tortured them. He also says that anybody that goes to fight in Vietnam is a sucker. My father believes it's important to look out for yourself first, then your family. He told me his solution was to put all of the Vietnamese that were friendly to us on a boat. Then carpet-bomb the whole country till it was just a big parking lot. Then sink the boat. We were on the couch and he had his arm over my shoulder. I thought he was serious until he started to laugh. "You're not a very nice man," my mother said. She wasn't as sick back then. My father poked me in the ribs. "I'm not a very nice man," he said.

"We should sniff spraypaint," Taro says. "You spray it in a bag, then you put the bag over your face."

"Sounds messy."

"It gets you high by killing brain cells."

"Feel that?"

"Feel what?"

"It's raining."

"It's not raining," Taro says. "Let's kidnap someone's kitten and hold it for ransom. How much should we ask for it?" When I don't answer he says, "Of course, we'd need a getaway vehicle."

"How about a fire truck?"

"I was thinking a go-kart," he says.

"I wonder if I should get home," I say. But it's still early. It won't be night for hours. I don't want to go home yet.

We head through the alleys to the schoolyard and hang out by the swings; the ground is rubber, made out of recycled gym shoes. "What do you think of Mrs. Smith?" Taro asks me.

"I wouldn't mind staying after school," I say. Everybody is in love with our teacher. My father even comes in for parent-teacher meetings. He tells me to tell Mrs. Smith he would like to take her for dinner sometime. He calls her a biscuit.

"She is fucking hot," Taro says. "I'm gonna fuck her."

"How are you going to do that? She's married."

"Marriage doesn't mean anything," Taro says, picking a scab at his ankle. "People just get married for tax reasons." I think about my mother and wonder if my father married her for tax reasons. It seems unlikely. "Guess what," he says. "My mother married my dad so she wouldn't get kicked out of the country."

"Really?" I say.

"Yeah. But don't tell anyone."

"Who would I tell?"

"Just don't, jackass."

We watch the older kids play basketball. Elvis, who's an American Indian, not an Indian Indian like the Indians on Devon, hits a shot from the three-point line and raises the back of his hands against his temples so it looks like he has wings on his head. If they need extra players they'll sometimes invite us to play with them. But they don't seem to want players today, even though the teams are uneven. Elvis is cool. One time we played with them and won and Elvis bought us a popsicle from the ice cream truck. Elvis looks over at us and raises the peace sign. We make the peace sign back to him. The two black kids, who live on the other side of Warren Park, are on Elvis's team, and they're beating the four white kids.

"I am totally gonna fuck Mrs. Smith," Taro says. I think of Mrs. Smith sitting at her desk in a dark blue shirt and the heels she wears.

"If you get someone pregnant before you're eighteen and they have a boy, would it be your brother or your son?" I ask.

"Your son, stupid."

"I know. I'm just kidding. What if you got your mom pregnant?"

"What are you, a hillbilly?"

"Well?"

"I don't even know why I hang out with you." Taro takes his cigarette pack out. "Last one." He lights his cigarette and smokes it for a while. I keep looking over at the other kids and wondering if we can get in the game. Elvis keeps hitting these crazy shots. It's like he can fly.

"Look at that," I say.

"My mom wants you to come over for dinner again." Taro hands me the smoke. His parents own a restaurant and they live in two rooms behind the restaurant. Nobody ever comes over to my house. Everybody in the neighborhood is afraid of my dad.

"For why?"

Taro shrugs. It's really starting to rain. "Seriously, though," Taro says. "I'm going to marry Mrs. Smith. And I want you to be my best man."

I think about it for a second. "I want to get married too. You can be my best man also," I say.

The building I live in is six stories high, the largest building on the block. It's grey and there's a small backyard but people throw trash back there and the high yellow weeds poke through the milk cartons and plastic bags. We live on the third floor. My father is the building manager, which means he collects the rents from everybody and sometimes evicts people. When he evicts people he wears his puffy black jacket with the policeman's patch on the shoulder. But my father is not a policeman. The building owner is short and Greek. His son, Aris, is in my grade and is good at bombardment. The owner comes over and my dad and him hang out in front of the building, leaning against my father's car, which is a blue Cougar convertible with a white leather interior. My dad is really proud of his car. He likes to stand in front of his car in the summer in just a pair of shorts and an undershirt he calls his wife-beater.

"You've been smoking," my mother says. She's lying on the couch, covered in her brown blanket with the tiger patterns on it. It's hard for her to talk so I don't answer. Next to her is a white bucket on the floor that she uses to go to the bathroom. It takes her a long time so she's careful not to drink too much water. There's a box of diapers waiting for her, but so far she has refused to wear them. Her head is shaking really hard from side to side. I'm worried her head will fall forward to her chest and she won't be able to get it up. I pick up the bucket, which has pee in it and toilet paper, and I walk it to the bathroom and dump it in the toilet and flush the toilet. Then I rinse it out in the bathtub. There is nothing that smells worse than this bucket when it's full of dark yellow pee. I let the warm water and soap rise in the bucket and press my forehead against the wall.

A few months ago I was hanging in front of the main door with Taro and some of the other guys. Taro was singing theme songs and everybody had to guess the TV show. My father stopped in the street and everybody got quiet and I ran down the steps and got in the car and we drove away. "Your mother's going to die soon," he said. He was wearing big-mirrored sunglasses so I saw myself instead of his eyes. It was a really sunny day out even though it was still cold. My dad drove with the top down. "I want you to be ready for it."

I kept my eyes on the dashboard, which is also white leather like the seats. My father stopped at a stop sign but didn't move right away. He was waiting for me to say something. I couldn't tell what the right answer was. I couldn't say OK. I wanted to ask, How? How was I supposed to be ready? "The doctors say it doesn't usually progress this fast. They don't know anything. See if you can find a doctor who can change an alternator." There was a car behind us, but they didn't honk. My father turned around and looked at them for a long second anyway. He put the car in park, resting his hand on the door window. I thought he was going to get out of the car. My dad's not afraid of anybody. Then he put the car back in gear and continued to drive.

My mother hasn't died yet, but she has gotten worse. She shakes all the time, even when she's sleeping. Sometimes I have to hold under her arms for her to pee. And she takes a lot of pills, which aren't supposed to make her better, just help her with the discomfort. My father says she got multiple sclerosis because where she's from there's a river named Ouse and a lot of people who lived along that river got multiple sclerosis. I go through the pictures my father keeps of her on the bookshelf. A picture taken at the McDonald's near Touhy shows my mother at the front of the line accepting a tray with a small hamburger and fries on it. She looks like someone just told her a joke. It must have been winter because she was wearing a fur hat that covered her ears. My mother, before, was incredibly beautiful. Everybody says so. She was always thin, but in the pictures she is very healthy looking. She never wore much makeup and her skin is clear except for a burst red blood vessel just below her eye. My father says she's descended from nobility, but my mother told me that wasn't true. Her father was a mailman. My father met her in England, in a small town near Sheffield. The story is that he was wearing a leather jacket at the time, and my mother had never met an American before. When he got back to the States he started writing her letters. Then he sent her a one-way ticket.

"I should never have married him," she said to me once after he had been screaming and the dining room table was broken into pieces, wood everywhere, half a table leg next to the couch. The curtains were torn down and there was broken glass on the floor. But she was already paralyzed by then. "I'm going to go into remission," she said. "Then I'm going to go home. You'll see."

I put the bucket back next to my mother. The streetlights have come on outside. I sit at the end of the couch with her and watch *The Price Is Right* with Bob Barker. He wants to know how much a trip to Bermuda is worth. Then he wants to know how much it costs for a box of Tide. Then he asks people to bid on Bermuda, the Tide, and an oil painting of some man sitting by the side of a pool. "The oil painting isn't worth anything. Two thousand dollars," I say. Bob Barker pulls a card out of an envelope. "Six thousand six hundred and eighty-three dollars," he says, and a woman in a thick white sweater jumps up and down, her hands clasped in front of her ample chest. The models in bathing suits are smiling and showing their wrists. "I guess that painting is worth more than I thought it was." I feel my mother's toes against my leg. I know I should stay home more. If something happens and I'm not here it's going to be my fault. I slide closer to her and her feet roll over my legs. I pull the blanket back and take her feet in my hands. I rub them back and forth as fast as I can, like I'm trying to start a fire. She likes it when I do this.

"Theo," she says, in that quavering way she has. But she doesn't want anything. She's just saying my name.

There are three bedrooms in our apartment. My bedroom is a small room just off the kitchen. There used to be wood paneling on the walls but my father covered it with wallpaper that looks like the sky, blue, with white clouds and birds. I love the wallpaper. It makes me feel like I'm outside, even when I'm sleeping.

My bed is next to the window and the rain is coming steadily now, hitting the glass like drumbeats. If I leave the shade up I can see the porch steps and the alley. If I lean my face into the glass I can see the basketball rim on Sammy and Edward's garage and the yard to the building across the way where the Germans keep a Great Dane. That's a big mean dog. I see a small orange glow down there. I wonder who's smoking in the alley in the rain. I have my history book in bed. Tomorrow we have a test on Andrew Jackson.

The back door opens. Then my father's heavy boots on the kitchen floor. I listen to hear if he is sighing. When my father is in a bad mood he sighs loudly. One time he was sighing so loudly that I opened my window and climbed three stories down the gutter to the street and didn't come back until the next day. The sound of the boots gets louder across the kitchen and then there is a knock on my door.

"Yes?" I say, as if it could be anybody.

"Come on out."

I slip out of my bed and pull on a pair of socks. My father sits at the kitchen table with the overhead light on. The light swings like the chain was yanked too hard. I look quickly to the sink to be sure that I've washed all the dishes already. There's a plate there, smeared with tomato sauce. There's a brown paper bag on the table. It reminds me of the bag full of money my father once invited me to look at.

He's seated with one arm on the table, another on his leg. He hasn't been shaving recently and his face is covered with thick grey stubble. My father has a thick face, with large cheeks hanging over his jaw like pouches. He's mostly bald with the rest of his hair cut short. He always has dark circles under his eyes but he never seems tired. He's wearing his brown leather jacket. I wonder if it's the same jacket he met my mother in. My mother is sleeping on the couch now. I used to wheel her into her bedroom. But now she says not to bother. She hasn't been off the couch in close to a week.

"Get two bowls and two spoons," my father says. I climb on the counter and grab two bowls and two spoons from the cabinet. Next to the bowls are ten cans of unopened Chef Boyardee. My father takes a small gun out of his pocket and places it on the table behind the bag. I sit down across from him. He reaches into the bag and pulls out a pint of vanilla ice cream. He balls up the bag and throws it toward the garbage but misses and the bag rolls near the refrigerator. "Pick that up later, OK?"

"OK."

He digs a spoon into the carton and dumps a big scoop of ice cream into a bowl and pushes the bowl toward me. Then he takes some for himself.

"How was your day? You taking care of yourself?"

"It was OK. I played with Edward and Sammy and then I hung out with Taro for a while."

"Oh yeah, Taro. The chink. Tell him your old man says hi."

"I will."

We eat the ice cream together quietly, my father drumming his large fingers on the table and the refrigerator buzzing. I can see the moon in the hatch window above the sink. The kitchen is very yellow. The floor and the refrigerator are both yellow. There's the door to the back porch, which is blue. But the white walls only reflect the floor and the refrigerator.

When the ice cream is almost done my father and I tip the bowls to our mouths and drink all of the stuff that has melted and place our bowls back down on the table together. He takes my bowl from me and places it inside his bowl and then the two spoons inside the top bowl together. He turns the gun on the table so it is pointing at me then places his hand over the gun, completely covering it. Then he puts the gun back in his pocket. He looks me up and down and bites on the inside of his mouth.

"How's everything at school?"

"It's good. We all wrote a report on black leaders. Then we put it together in a black leader book. I wrote about Jesse Jackson."

My father nods and smiles. "I could tell you a couple of things about your pal Jesse Jackson." He leans forward and rubs my head. Then leans back and looks at me. I lean back too; we both place an elbow on the table. "So everything's good? Nobody's giving you a hard time?"

"Nobody gives me a hard time."

"What a night for it to start raining. They're teaching Jesse Jackson in schools now. Times sure have changed. You need some money or something? Here, take ten dollars." My father pulls out a large wad of bills from his pocket. He likes to have a lot of cash on him. If he gets arrested he wants to be able to make bail. He peels through the bills, like he's considering giving me more, and then pulls a ten-dollar bill off the bottom of the stack, hands it to me. He puts the roll of money back in his pocket. "Everything's good?" he asks me again. He looks a little suspicious this time. I wonder if he's going to ask for the ten dollars back.

"Yeah," I tell him. I fold the ten-dollar bill in half and put it in my pocket. My father's eyes widen and close. He raises his hand and I flinch. He squeezes the skin on his forehead and I think he's going to cry.

Somewhere on my block a car's motor is still running. He's going back outside again. He reaches across the table and rubs his hands beneath my nose, squeezing whatever he got into a fist, then wipes his hand on his jeans.

"You're a handsome guy," he says. "Anybody ever tell you that?"

I don't answer but I feel the heat in my face. He pushes against the table, his chair leg scraping the floor. He stands, patting his pockets, making sure he has everything. I stand with him, gathering the dishes.

"Alright," he says, latching a ring full of keys to a clip on his belt. "You're Daddy's boy. Don't worry about anything else."

His arms encircle me, pulling me into him, surrounding me with the hard dark creases of his jacket and his smell, which is thick, like metal and oil. He stands still. I'm with him, holding the empty bowls. When a horn punctures the quiet apartment, my father grips my ribs. He hasn't left yet. He's still here.

ACKNOWLEDGMENTS

I'd like to first thank Tamara Guirado for encouraging me to write about sex; as ridiculous as that sounds, it's true. I owe a tremendous debt to the Truman Capote Foundation for funding the fellowship at Stanford that allowed me to write this book.

Tom Kealey and Thomas McNeely gave many thoughtful readings and provided incredible insight. They are the two greatest readers in the world and I'm keeping them forever. Elizabeth Tallent, John L'Heureux, David MacDonald and Tobias Wolff have been my mentors for the past two years and I've profited from their wisdom. I would have written this from an asylum if not for Gay Pierce, my surrogate grandmother and therapist, who never told me to go away, even when she had work to do.

I would also like to thank David Poindexter, who let me know that I could write whatever I wanted and he would publish it as long as it was good; Dave Eggers for making this a better book with his incredibly skillful editing; Eli Horowitz, Suzanne Kleid, Gideon Lewis-Kraus, Tommy Thornhill, and the rest of the crew at McSweeney's and 826 Valencia. Finally, I'd like to thank Chris Cooney, Andrew Miller, Christine Fox, Chris Donahue, Erik Jensen, Wendy McKennon, Abigail Martin, Karina Arambula, Alice Poon, Julie Brannegan, Jeremiah Johnson, Jon Berry, and Ben Peterson, because good friends matter more than anything else.

ABOUT THE AUTHOR

Stephen Elliott lives in San Francisco and lectures at Stanford University. He recently edited *Politically Inspired*, a collection of fiction shaped by current events. He was born in Chicago, and was a Ward of the Court from the ages of thirteen to eighteen. This is his fourth novel.

www.stephenelliott.com